Borrowed, Not Lost

LOOKING GLASS SAGA

BOOK THREE

Borrowed, Not Lost

TANYA LISLE

SCRAP PAPER ENTERTAINMENT

ISBN-13: 978-1-988911-69-4

Scrap Paper Entertainment
www.scrappaperentertainment.com

Contents

CHAPTER 1

Hiding a Cook in the Kitchen

BEING GROUNDED HAD never come at a better time.

Alice had spent more time in Wonderland than her room since summer began. As soon as she was home and far away from the Bandersnatch, she was able to go through the mirror and into Wonderland again. As soon as she could, she started to look for where Mike, Mark and Matt had gone. She was hopeful and began scouring the place as much she could, looking through all the familiar areas, and a few not so familiar ones, for any sign of them.

Every night she donned her watch to keep an eye on how long she'd been gone, so that she could return before she was missed. The time wouldn't move while she was watching it, but changed as soon as she looked away. Alice was quickly learning how time worked in Wonderland — which was not very well — but it was often convenient enough to allow her to finish looking before she had to return home.

After a week, Alice was running out of places to look. She combed as much of Wonderland as she could while avoiding anyone who knew her, and therefore avoided any lectures about her rudeness that might cut into her searching time. Now she was starting to run out of people she didn't know.

She didn't remember Wonderland being this big before. It had always been kind of large and mysterious, but the first time she was here she spent most of it as large as a ladybug. It occurred to her that the brothers may have been shrunk as well, and soon she'd have to try becoming very small in order to continue looking, but she could still come up with a few places she could look before resorting to that.

There were also a few people that she would absolutely need to ask before she went changing sizes. While Cat would know for certain, he was no longer in Wonderland. The Mad Hatter was missing as far as she could tell. At least, she hadn't run across him or his tea party yet. There was still the Caterpillar. He might know where she could find something. He seemed to know far more than he should when she was a child, and she could only hope that he still did.

It was surprising how many mushroom patches there were in Wonderland, but it was easy to find the one with the smoke coming out of it. She stepped away thinking about the Caterpillar's hookah and, when she appeared, the smoking mushroom patch was down below, billowing out blue and green smoke in small puffs.

Alice bent down to peer into the underbrush and find the Caterpillar there, looking not at all bothered by Alice's sudden appearance or the parting of the foliage above him. Instead, he took another puff and nodded up to her, waiting for her to begin the encounter herself.

"Hello, Caterpillar," she said, glad that she wasn't met with how rude she was for once. "It's been a while. How have you been?"

He took a long, contemplative puff on his hookah and let out a fluttering trail of purple and blue smoke. "Alice," he said, letting her name roll over her tongue like a distant memory. "Hello. It has been a while since your last visit. Are you only passing through once more?"

"Passing through again, I'm afraid," Alice said. She sat down so that she could easier talk to him. She had been so small the last time she saw him, but even at her full size, he was still an enormous bug. "I've lost a few people. Perhaps you've seen them pass through here." Alice stopped, waiting for an answer before realizing she never asked a question. "Have you seen three boys around here? They're a little older than I am. Dark hair. Taller. They all look the same."

"I cannot say that I have," the Caterpillar said, taking another long puff of his hookah. Alice thought she saw this puff of orange and yellow linger behind him and settle into wings on his back before fading away. "Not truthfully, in any event. I suppose the words would still come and form, but words with no truth are not worth speaking at all, now are they?"

Alice would have argued that if she wasn't trying to find people. Words with no truth to them was precisely how she had won so much of the freedom she had right now. Not that aimlessly looking around Wonderland for lost boys was what she'd thought of when she thought of freedom.

The Caterpillar took another puff and Alice stayed quiet. He was going to say more and she knew better than to stop the Caterpillar from speaking when she needed information.

"I may have seen one peculiar thing," he said after a far too long pause. "There was the most peculiar foot. It would have crushed me had I been under it. Very inconsiderate, I thought, but it was so odd that I continued to watch it. There was one boy attached to it, constantly crushing several things underfoot. Did not stay on the path where feet will not crush things."

He looked pointedly at Alice's feet; she was grateful they were on a rock. Luck on her side at last. She stayed quiet as he returned to his hookah and his story.

"He was running away from a red metal boot. I had thought he was a little familiar, like I had seen a shoe like his before. The first one, not the metal one. The metal one was always meant to crush things, but I do not know about the other one. The other one, that boy attached to him kept yelling all sorts of things at the red boot. Not very polite things. A bit like you, Alice. But the red one caught the strange one soon enough, and the red one took him away."

"A red metal boot?" Alice asked. Her heart clenched in her chest at that. She had a sinking feeling about this. "Did this boot belong to a large set of red metal armour by chance?"

"So you *do* know who I'm talking about!" the Caterpillar said. "Quite a lovely boot, though. Very shiny. If only it didn't crush so many things."

"Thank you," Alice said, though she wasn't happy about what she'd found. He was at the castle. Alice really didn't want to go to the castle.

Alice bid the Caterpillar a fond farewell. "If you're heading to the castle," he said as she started to get up, "could you take these with you?" He gestured to the mushrooms in a patch near him. "I haven't been able to deliver them myself, but I think the Queen of Hearts could do with a little perspective."

Alice grinned and picked a few of them, not at all against putting a few of them into the Queen's soup. Unlike the cake and the potion, she knew the Caterpillar's brand of mushrooms had a bit more unruly and unpredictable effect on anyone who ate them. She would very much like to see the slender queen with her head on the top of a very long neck that she couldn't quite keep upright.

And then the image of it started to blend into the memory of the Queen's melted face. Alice vowed to avoid the Queen of Hearts at all costs this time around.

She checked her watch to make sure she had time for it and tried to think of a place in the castle where she would arouse the least suspicion if she appeared. A place where the Queen and the Red Knight would not be. When she couldn't come up with a place, she opted to start from the bottom and work her way up.

She walked forward into the dungeons, finding the Jail Bird napping in the corner and people in the cages. In fact, there were several people who looked a little irritated, all in one cell that had grown to absorb all the cells on one side. She stopped and looked into it, blinking as she tried to come up with some explanation for it, or something more intelligent and polite to say. Instead, there was only one thought on her mind.

"Do you bring the tea party with you everywhere?"

The Mad Hatter perked up in the cell. He had obviously tried and failed to be a good host to his more dour guests who realized the gravity of the situation more than he did. The tea was likely cold and there wasn't actually a table there at all. They'd taken apart a wall that separated the cells to turn into a table. Even the cups were made out of bricks and Alice assumed that, since everything was brick, there probably wasn't even any tea here.

"Why Alice!" the Mad Hatter said, clapping his hands and looking at her through the bars. "How lovely to see you, dear. But you can't join the party this time. Invite only, I'm afraid, though you would be a lot more interesting than these ones. Quite a dull lot, they are. No conversation. No manners. Well, better than yours. At least they don't interrupt my stories."

Alice looked past him to see that some of these people weren't from Wonderland. There was a certain look that Wonderland had to their inhabitants that Alice hadn't noticed until someone who wasn't from there scowled at her from behind the bars of a Wonderland jail cell. The people of Wonderland, those who hadn't had their hearts removed, had much brighter eyes. But these others, they looked down and upset. One was just a boy who looked like he was about to cry.

"I understand," Alice said, looking back at the party. None of them looked back at her. The people not from Wonderland bothered her. What else had been getting through and where had they come from? She worried that Cat had let even more people through, but they didn't look like they were from Lucena Academy either. They were from somewhere new.

"Oh good," the Mad Hatter said.

"Why are you here?"

"Because we were caught, of course!" he said as if it were the most obvious thing in all of Wonderland. "When you are caught doing something that you aren't supposed to do, people do not want to have tea! Upsetting, that. But you know the Queen of Hearts. Still upset that she doesn't have a pretty daughter yet. Perhaps you should offer, Alice. She does seem to quite like you."

"I don't think that will work out," Alice said. He'd forgotten the last time already hadn't he?

"Well, think on it," he said. "You did not before, but perhaps you might like the idea more now. You have gotten older, you see, and time will change you. You will grow your hair longer and perhaps you will want to become a princess as well."

So he did remember.

"What did you do that was so bad that you were caught and thrown in jail?" Alice asked. She shouldn't even bother asking. She should be looking for the shoe the Caterpillar had seen.

"Oh, that," the Mad Hatter said, waving it off. "I found them! The White King and that blasted Hare. They've been hiding in the castle this whole time! Just off peeling potatoes instead of doing what they were supposed to do, the both of them. Unfortunately, they are quite good at peeling potatoes. The Queen of Hearts would not part with them."

At least he was taking this unnaturally well.

"She won't let any of us leave, though," he said. "A shame. It's getting so crowded in here and I fear that there won't be enough tea for everyone if she keeps throwing people in."

"There's no tea in here now!" the little boy yelled at him, floating in the air as he said so. He was immediately shushed by the other more dour looking inhabitants as a futile gesture and pulled back down into his seat.

"Such rudeness at my tea party," the Mad Hatter said. "But a guest is a guest is a guest! Although I do hope they come soon to take another one away. It might mean we will have room for you as well! But, you know, you would need to join us in here. And it would mean someone else was sent to see the Queen. The last one has not come back to visit yet. What did he say his name was?"

"Lance," the boy said, sniffling as the tears started to well up in his eyes and pour over. "He was nice, but now they said they were going to take his heart."

Alice's heart sank. She was already too late.

"There is a much bigger concern here than that," the Mad Hatter said. "Lance will live on without his heart, but I fear I have been unable to feed the Jabberwocky for quite a while. The poor dear will get so hungry without me to feed him scones and a nice cup of tea. Perhaps, Alice, since you are not invited, you might check up on the poor creature?"

Alice looked at him and tried to decide if she could get away with smacking him without waking the Jail Bird up. He didn't seem to be paying any attention. "You want me to go feed your Jabberwocky?" she asked.

The creature did not like her, to say the least. She'd brought him to Wonderland with a great amount of difficulty and the Jabberwocky had never been willing to let her get close. She might have even been eaten by the thing if she weren't as careful as she was.

"If you would be so kind, dear," the Mad Hatter said. "We know you aren't busy, seeing as you are here."

"The Jabberwocky hates me."

"Well, maybe if you bathed a little more thoroughly," the Mad Hatter suggested. "He likes very few people, but so few people bathe regularly that it's hardly a wonder! I imagine you smell like a barbarian to him and no one wants to associate with someone so uncivilized as that. Ah, but here, this should help to cover the smell."

Alice was not at all surprised to find there was another hat under the Mad Hatter's hat, though this one was quite a bit smaller. He passed his larger hat through the cell bars and

Alice took it, not really sure what he thought she should do with it.

"Now, mind you are good to it," the Mad Hatter said. "It is quite dear to me, that hat. But the Jabberwocky, he only knows me by it. My good smell should cover your bad one and he'll let you near enough to take care of him for me."

She put it on, which made the Mad Hatter happy. It was too big on her and dropped over her eyes, leaving her in the dark. She managed to tilt it back up, resting it on her head like a hood, and looked back at the Mad Hatter, who was beaming. "Much better! Much better! So much better than a silly old black ribbon, wouldn't you say? Now run along. He needs to be taken care of, the poor thing."

Alice stared at him and then past him to the crying boy at the table.

"Isn't anyone going to come save us?" he cried. "I don't like it here. I want to go back home! I'll even let a girl save me if I have to! There's nothing to eat or drink and he's crazy!"

"Saved from a party, really," the Mad Hatter said. "Alice, you are the only other person I have ever met that was so rude. I do hope the Queen of Hearts takes him next."

Alice took out a couple of the mushrooms from the Caterpillar and threw them through the bars to land on the table. If he was that hungry and wanted out, maybe the mushrooms would help him, but she didn't want to be in the presence of the Mad Hatter anymore. She walked away and went to the next place she could think of.

She was surrounded by trees a moment later, all of them with pots and pans hanging off them, along with forks and spoons. A small bush grew butter knives and far more mature butcher's knives. There were fridges and all sorts of other things for the kitchen growing around her and she stayed well near the back to think.

Lance was Mike and Mike had been taken to the Queen of Hearts. Maybe he would just be without a heart and not dead from having it removed. She really didn't know how that worked for people outside of Wonderland who didn't have the madness to keep them together. When you stole a heart from someone who was from Wonderland, you took away their madness and turned them into an obedient servant to the Queen of Hearts, presumably because she was the one who held your heart. But if you took someone's heart out in the real world, then they were usually dead.

Somehow, she couldn't fathom anyone dying in Wonderland. It was dangerous and heads might have been removed now and then, but no one ever really died here. She didn't know what she would do if she found out he was dead. She did her best to not think about it. There was hope. A chance. There had to be.

Alice heard a branch snap and perked up. Mindless drones

though they were, she still didn't want to know what would happen if they caught her right now. She almost hid in the knife bush, but quickly settled for one that was flowering pretty little tea cups and saucers instead.

A boy with dark hair and a perfectly intact chest came down, moving mechanically as he looked around the small forest for something. Alice's breath caught in her throat. He was alive. One of them was at least. She didn't know quite which one for sure yet, but one of them was definitely still alive. No mole on his palm, so not Matt.

He went to the knife bush and Alice risked coming out of her hiding spot and pouncing on him. She grabbed him around the mouth in case he tried to scream. He jumped under her hands and thrashed, pushing Alice back until she clattered into the teacup bush.

"Alice?" he demanded in a harsh whisper, the mechanical movements becoming more natural as he turned on her and went to help her up. "What are you doing here? You can't be here!"

"I'm getting you out," Alice told him. "Come on, we just need to find a shiny pan."

"What?" he asked before shaking his head. "You can't be here. Do you know what they do to people in here?"

"I know exactly what they do here," Alice said. "That's why we need to go. Now. Come on."

"How did you get here?"

"What part of we need to leave right now do you not understand?" Alice demanded of him, keeping her voice as low as his. "It's amazing the Queen of Hearts didn't take your heart already. Did she take your heart?"

"How do you know about any of this?" he asked. "Wait, are you the Alice that the Mad Hatter kept talking about? He said something about a really rude girl that came to his tea party and didn't want to be a princess."

"If you met the Queen of Hearts, you wouldn't want to be her daughter either," Alice told him. "Now, we have to-"

"I found the Hare and the White King, though," he said. "I think we can get them out."

"Wonderland is getting to you," Alice said desperately, grabbing his hand and trying to pull him to the pots. "Come on, we have to get you out of here. Adrianna's worried. Everyone's worried. You didn't leave with them at the end of the year and I had to tell Adrianna that I lost you guys and I promised I'd get you guys back as soon as I could."

"But I can't go yet," Mike said, pulling his hand away. "I said I'd try to find the Hare and the White King and get them out if I could."

"You know he's mad, right? The Mad Hatter? It's in his name."

"He also helped me," Mike said. "He told me how to keep

from getting my heart ripped out. Well, he kind of told me. I owe him. I can't go until I help him get out and help him get them out too."

"I can come back and do that later," Alice said. "For now, you need to-"

Alice stopped, both of them turning to see something step into the woods. Red armour filled the small path and he caught sight of Alice almost immediately. She pulled on Mike's arm, but he became a mechanical zombie again. He looked at Alice as if he expected her to do the same.

She checked her watch. She didn't have time.

"The Queen of Hearts wants you," the Red Knight said, raising his weapon.

Alice took a quick look at Mike, who was frozen and staring at the sword. Distraction. She needed to get him away from Mike. Or Lance. Whatever his name was now. Easily done.

Alice pressed the remaining bag of mushrooms into Mike's hand, hoping he'd figure out what to do with them, and slid back around the tree. She showed up behind the red knight. Maybe he could cause a little chaos and slip out on his own before she got back, but she wasn't counting on it.

"She wants me?" Alice asked the Red Knight. "Tell her I don't really want to see her."

"You will come with me," the Red Knight said, turning around.

Alice ran across the trees and behind another one, appearing up in the branches and waiting for the Red Knight to follow her. He did, so predictably, as soon as she talked. "I don't particularly want to come with you," she said. "It seems like it would not be in my best interest."

"Your interest does not concern the Queen."

Alice appeared above him in a tree full of chrome fridges. She looked around, but Mike was already gone. At least she knew where he was. Next time, she could get him back if he didn't manage to escape on his own. Whatever she had to do.

First, she needed to get back home before she was missed. She'd be back.

Alice reached over and grabbed a knife out of the knife bush, then severed the chrome fridge from the branch. It dropped down on the knight, this time with a good bit of weight, and looked like it was going to pin him down. Alice looked at the reflective surface and jumped down onto the fridge, falling through it and back into her own room.

CHAPTER 2

Home Life

ALICE ROLLED OUT on the floor and got to her feet, running to check her bedroom door. Still locked. Outside, she could hear yelling coming from downstairs, followed by dead silence and the front door closing. Her father had just left for work that day and her mother would be up to see her in a few minutes.

Alice quickly changed back into her pajamas, throwing the Mad Hatter's hat into the corner of her room, and threw herself under the covers.

Right on time, there was a knock on her door. "Alice?" her mother asked from the other side of it. The lock clicked and she let herself in. Alice pretended to wake up. "Alice, I'm going to work now," she said, sitting on the side of Alice's bed. "Ms. Miller will be by to look in on you in a few hours."

"Okay," Alice said, trying to make herself seem as tired

as she could manage. It was strange. The more time she spent in Wonderland — and she spent a lot of time in Wonderland — the less tired she was. At first, anyway. "Have a good day at work."

Her mother left without another word. Alice waited under the covers until she heard the front door close a second time before she got out of bed and jumped into the shower to wash the sweat of Wonderland off of her.

She was through with her shower quickly and went down to the kitchen for something to eat. Before, being grounded was awful because she was so often hungry. Her parents, to make sure she didn't get out into the house and to the television or computers without them around, made sure her door locked from the outside to keep her in her room. This usually meant that she didn't get breakfast because she slept too late to join her parents, whose breakfast consisted entirely of a cup of coffee. When Lori was around, she would make sure Alice got food, but without her, Alice doubted her parents remembered to keep anything around for breakfast.

Now, though, it was much better. After a trip to Wonderland, she was usually hungry for something. Thanks to the treacle, she could reach into the cupboards without opening them, and she was able to fix herself a quick snack while sitting directly beneath the cameras so that her father would not catch her out of her room. He wouldn't be watching now, still on his way to the office, but she learned to be cautious about it well before they put the lock on her room.

It was nice being out of her room for a while. Under the camera, she could still see the backyard. It was sprawling and wide in the bright sun with the creek down at the edge. She'd fallen into Wonderland there the first time and hadn't been allowed to venture that far out on her own since. Ms. Miller still let her wander off on her own once in a while, but usually when they went anywhere that wasn't in the house or on the large grounds.

When Alice was done, she dropped her dishes in the sink to clean when Ms. Miller arrived and went up to her room. Once she was there, she dropped into a dreamless slumber. She was fine the first couple of nights she went to Wonderland, but she found the more often she went, the more tired she was an hour or two after she got back. Fatigue didn't happen in Wonderland, but here, a whole night without sleep really took its toll.

Ms. Miller shook her awake several hours later. Alice looked at her clock, seeing it read one in the afternoon. About five hours of sleep. That was fine by her.

"Morning, sunshine," Ms. Miller said, smiling underneath her round glasses. She went around to her window and flung open the curtains. "You've been sleeping a lot lately. Late nights?"

"You could say that," Alice said. She liked Ms. Miller. She'd been her tutor for the past couple years and was probably the only person Alice could count on without Lori around. She knew about Alice's time in Wonderland, though she didn't believe it and never asked about it. She was brought on as a personal tutor and counsellor for Alice, but had long ago determined Alice was perfectly sane and didn't need to be put on any medication. With Lori teaching her to just not talk about Wonderland and Ms. Miller implying the same thing, they'd gotten Alice all the freedom she needed. Except for now.

"You know, this is a little too extreme for a grounding," Ms. Miller said again, as she did every morning. Alice got out of bed and went to the bathroom to change while Ms. Miller set down a pack of books for Alice to read. "What did you do again?"

"They caught me out of bed after curfew."

"Trespassing, wasn't it?"

"The school was unlocked," Alice insisted, coming out in a shirt and shorts. "They said it was fine."

"Right, with two boys," Ms. Miller said, grinning. "You're lucky your father didn't pull you out of school entirely, you know, but he's got a few other things on his mind right now."

Alice nodded, though she didn't need to say anything else. She knew her parents were fighting. She wondered if it was about her again, but knew better than to worry about that. Ms. Miller had already been through it with her when she was younger. Alice understood that whatever happened between her parents wasn't something that she could stop and it was not her fault.

"They're really loud in the morning," Alice said.

"Are they remembering to get you breakfast this time?"

"Yes," Alice lied. There was a bowl in the sink downstairs to corroborate her story. No need for Ms. Miller to get any more worried about her. She always worried so much whenever Alice was grounded for saying or doing anything.

"What about dinner?"

"Sometimes." That was a little trickier. Sometimes she would be let out of her room to join them for dinner, but sometimes they would argue so much that they didn't eat at all. Sometimes they would go out together. Sometimes they were in the office so late that they didn't bother with dinner. Not that it mattered too much, because Ms. Miller had resources for it already.

She opened the bag she brought with her and pulled out a grocery bag to throw into Alice's bottom drawer. It contained five apples and a box of granola bars, like she brought once a week for Alice to snack on when she got too hungry.

"I swear, if I thought I could I would call your parents for child endangerment," she said, turning back around to look Alice over. "You are definitely losing weight. And you shouldn't be. You're still growing."

Alice thought that might be because she was spending so much time running around Wonderland trying to fix her mistakes, but she knew she shouldn't mention that.

Instead, she shrugged and took one of the books off the top of the stack that Ms. Miller had brought her. The cover was of a history textbook. Inside, she could tell it wasn't one. "What's this?"

"*Harry Potter*," Ms. Miller said. "It's about a boy who finds out he's really a wizard and gets swept up in a magical world. It's not in the curriculum."

"Am I allowed?" Alice asked, suddenly feeling like she should put it back down in case this turned out to be a test.

"I think your parents are a bit too busy to worry about what you're reading," Ms. Miller said. "Besides, I think you're old enough to know the difference between fiction and reality. And you're going to be getting access the internet at school soon. Once you have that, they aren't going to be able to keep you from reading whatever you want."

Ms. Miller smiled a giddy smile, like she did when she got her way. "I'll leave a couple of them with you tonight and tomorrow you can tell me which ones you want to continue with over the rest of the summer, okay? I want you to read for fun without having to learn something."

Alice nodded, though wasn't sure what any of this was about. She wasn't going to argue, though. They certainly looked a lot more entertaining and enjoyable than the text-books that she had been relying on. Alice put them in her top drawer, though left *Harry Potter* out so she could read it today.

"What do you want for lunch today? Something nice and big."

Alice shrugged, Ms. Miller waving her off and smiling. "I'll come up with something. From that call this morning, I don't think your parents are going to be back until late tonight."

"Shouldn't we go over things for next semester?" Alice asked.

"You've been through the material already," Ms. Miller said, pointing out the books on her shelf. "I don't know what you're going to have for English, but we've already been through most of the material until you hit grade eleven. Now, I want you to try and get through at least the first chapter of that book and tell me what you think by the time I get back."

"And if I finish a chapter?" Alice asked.

"Then if you like it, keep reading. If you don't, move on to the next one. Try to give them all more than a chapter, though."

Ms. Miller left her there, closing the door and fiddling with the lock on the other side of the door. She never actually locked the door like her parents did. She just pretended for the camera out in the hall. Alice knew better than Ms. Miller where all the cameras were and what the game they were playing was. Ms. Miller was paid only to check on Alice and be there for a couple hours so that her father wouldn't have to pay her too much when Alice was grounded. It was to make Alice feel worse about getting in trouble because she was affecting Ms. Miller's paycheck.

Except Ms. Miller didn't care. She had other kids to cover her expenses.

Alice sat at her desk and started to read about Harry Potter, a poor boy who was left in a cupboard under the stairs and servant to his mean aunt, uncle and cousin, none of whom liked him very much. She was four chapters in by the time Ms. Miller brought up a large plate of lasagna for Alice to finish over the next hour.

"Well?" she asked.

"Thank you!" Alice said, diving into the lasagna with earnest. She knew better than to finish it all right away, keeping half of it for later in a small Tupperware in her bottom drawer. Dinner and lunch in one, because Ms. Miller was worried she wasn't getting enough to eat.

"And how's the book?" she asked.

"I like it so far," Alice said. "But I don't know why he doesn't run away if it's that terrible there. It's not like they locked him in that closet really even. He could just walk out the front door and try to find somewhere better."

"Well, Alice, why don't you run away?" Ms. Miller asked. "You've been locked in this room, but you have a way out. You could leave, but you don't."

Alice followed Ms. Miller's eyes to under her bed where a rope sat in a box, hidden away where her parents had yet to find it. She had brought it the first time Alice was grounded and Lori begged her to help Alice find a way out. The next day, Ms. Miller came with a rope long enough for Alice to tie to one of her bed posts and dangle out her window, then down to the ground. There was also a number in the box for Ms. Miller and her solemn word that she would come to find Alice wherever she was if she ever needed it. Alice didn't need that number. She'd memorized it long ago.

Alice thought on it for a moment, but she could only think of why *she* didn't leave when she had a way out right under her bed. "He doesn't have anywhere else to go?" Alice suggested. "He doesn't know anyone else except for the Dursleys and he doesn't have any money to take a taxi somewhere else. And no one's going to believe him if he does tell someone, so he stays because he doesn't know what else to do."

Ms. Miller nodded. "Good reasoning. That might be it. Did you want to keep reading it for today?"

"Yes please," Alice said. Having an actual story to read

for fun was amazing. Sure, Ms. Miller was probably going to ask her about it when she came back tomorrow, but it meant she didn't have to read another book about animals or biology or chemical compounds or theories of something. It was like watching *Back to the Future* or that movie marathon she went on over spring break. "Can I keep reading it?"

Ms. Miller smiled. "Of course. I need to clean, but I'll be back before I go, okay?"

Alice smiled as she sat down and went back to the book. The strange new Wizarding World was so much nicer than Wonderland. She found herself a little jealous of Harry for finding a world where everyone liked him so much and school where he found friends so easily. She reminded herself that he had apparently saved the wizarding world, so they probably liked him in part for his fame, but it all came so easily after he went there.

Harry didn't have Cat following him around and trying to make him read a book that drove people crazy. He just had to sit still while a hat told him where he was supposed to go and teachers around that would tell him what to do. He had it a lot easier than Alice. He better almost die by the end of this to make it up to her.

Ms. Miller came back just as Harry got sorted into Gryffindor, though Alice barely noticed. She looked up as soon as Ms. Miller tapped her on the shoulder, looking back around to see her smiling. "I'm done for today," she said. "I need to lock up. How's the book?"

"I like it," Alice said. "Everything got really easy for him when he found out he was magic."

"It won't stay easy," Ms. Miller said, grinning and she looked down at the book. "I'll bring the second and third books for you tomorrow. Try not to stay up too late reading them."

Alice smiled. "I won't," she said. She was intending on staying up late for different reasons.

"How long are you going to have to stay in here, again?" Ms. Miller asked. "Another week of being grounded, right?"

"Until the end of next week," Alice agreed.

"We're going somewhere on the first day you're released. Amusement park. Roller coasters everywhere. It will be very educational. Physics and all that."

This time when Ms. Miller left, she actually locked Alice's door behind her. When she was gone, Alice went back to the book and let herself get lost in it. It was exactly what her parents had always banned her from doing, what kept her from going into the library for anything recreational, and what made her hesitate when movie nights were brought up.

Movie nights made her sad now. Sarah had gone missing on a movie night and the promise of a *Lord of the Rings* marathon movie day with friends now carried that sour taste of knowing that Sarah would have wanted to be there. Adrianna didn't remember her, nor did anyone else at all. Alice needed to figure out how to make the Bandersnatch give her back.

Alice finished *Harry Potter and the Philosopher's Stone* before her parents got home that night, which left her time to come up with a plan. She knew where Mike was, so she just had to get him out. He didn't want to leave until he got the Mad Hatter, the March Hare and the White King out. There was absolutely no mention of getting anyone out with their heart, which should make the rescue attempt easier.

And she still had the Mad Hatter's hat. Her mind was spinning with the potential ideas, each a little crazier than the last. Which, in the case of Wonderland, was likely a good thing.

Her parents were in after nine, which meant they wouldn't be in to check on her. She'd finished her dinner an hour ago and she waited until their tired footsteps shuffled into their own room at the end of the hall before she started to get her things together.

Equipped with her watch, a good pair of shoes for the running she'd likely be doing, and a mirror that reflected Wonderland, she waited. A minute passed. Then two. Her watch ticked down until half an hour with no sound from her parents room passed.

She hoped this would work as she climbed up onto her dresser and stepped through the mirror into Wonderland.

CHAPTER 3

Prison Break

THE JABBERWOCKY WAS easy to find. He curled up on the table of the Mad Hatter's original tea party that Alice had first visited so long ago. Asleep was one way that she liked the Jabberwocky, but it was a restless one, as his tail kept twitching. Underneath the table, the Dormouse was also asleep under a fallen cup.

Okay, time to put the suicidal plan into action.

Alice put the Mad Hatter's hat on her head, balancing it so that it didn't fall over her face. She knew it was going to, but for now she wanted her hands free and as much of his scent on her as she could manage. Maybe it would be enough to keep the Jabberwocky from turning Alice into lunch.

"Hey," she called, getting closer to the Jabberwocky, but not within swiping range. "Jabberwocky! Wake up!"

One eye opened, then the other, both of them rounding

on Alice. He looked enraged at Alice disturbing his slumber, but that abated quickly as his nostrils flared and took in a strange yet familiar scent. His eyes were on the hat and he went closer for another smell. His wings folded back down and he appeared to be docile as he studied the hat.

She stepped back, vanishing from her spot and appearing several feet away. The Jabberwocky shot up, looking around for where the hat went. He turned to where she was now, looking at the hat on her head curiously again and following it.

If she had the patience, she might have done this the whole way, but the castle was a bit of a walk from here. She took another step and appeared half way between the Jabberwocky's current location and the castle. She hadn't forgotten her short cut. With the Jabberwocky firmly in her mind, she yelled out, "*Ábedecian bealu gásric ælwiht hércyme!*"

From the trees, the dragon burst out the top with his wings spread at their full length. It was good to know that those wings were fully functional, but she was sure someone would notice the large, dark creature crawling through the sky towards the castle. She needed to get moving and make sure everyone was in on this plan.

A few steps later, she appeared in the kitchen. Mike was easy to spot in the crowd, thankfully, and after stepping to the side, she was peering over Mike's shoulder, looking down at the water he was stirring. It was bubbling, but as near as Alice could tell, there wasn't anything in the pot besides water. Casually, he dropped a single mushroom from inside his sleeve and continued to stir.

"Looks good," Alice said, stepping the rest of the way around him.

He jumped and turned to her, grabbing at his chest and looking wildly around. "Alice!" he hissed. "What are you doing here?"

"I'm going to break you out," she said, her own eyes darting around. No sign of the Red Knight or any guards in the kitchen so far. She might have a minute before she had to leave again.

"I can't go until—"

"Breaking them out too. Just get them together and be ready to go."

"Ready for what?"

Alice saw a flash of red by the door. "For the dragon. Gotta go."

"The *what?*"

Alice went back out to the gardens. There were plenty of people walking around all through the gardens, so she moved to the roof. There were blank cards crawling all over the place, through every inch of the maze and around the former lawn golf field. The porcupines walked and stopped while the flamingos followed them around, none of them sure what to do with themselves now that they were not only heartless, but without a proper game to play.

She knew where she was going next, so she fixed the hat on her head again and looked up to the sky. She hoped that he would hear her from here. With the Jabberwocky in her mind again, she yelled from the rooftop, "*Ábedecian bealu gásric ælwiht hércyme!*"

A call from below let her know that they noticed. She looked down to see the playing cards advancing on the tower, some already starting to climb up the wall and come after her.

Out in the distance, Alice could see a dark speck crawling through the sky and quickly getting closer. She let out a sigh of relief that the spell still worked from that far away. Everything was about to get a little crazy and she needed to be quick.

Alice spun around and left, appearing down in the dungeons. So far, she was finding that the crazier the idea and the looser the plan, the better it worked in Wonderland. So long as she didn't expect anyone to be nice to her today, she might just be able to pull this off.

The dungeon was much like she had left it. The Jail Bird was still sleeping in the corner and the Mad Hatter was still trying to have a pleasant party. The difference was now the young boy was curled up in the corner and staring straight ahead, his legs a little longer than before and he was staring dead ahead without deviating. Alice could handle that, as there was only one person that she wanted to speak to in there and no one else looked like they wanted to chat. In fact, most of them were glaring at her when she came in.

"Hello Hatter," Alice said in greeting, pushing the hat up off her eyes as it started to droop. "I do hope the party has almost come to a close. You are going to leave soon."

"Is someone coming for his heart?" one of the men behind him asked. Now that Alice looked, she could swear it was an older man dressed as a pirate.

"No one's coming for anyone's heart," Alice said. "We're breaking out."

"Pardon us if we're not quite believing you, Miss," the pirate said, glancing to the boy in the corner. "Your last bit of help didn't turn out so well."

"Yeah, the mushrooms are a little tricky," Alice said. "I'm sorry about that. I probably should have warned you about the Caterpillar's particular stock before leaving them with you. But he looks all right."

"Ah, you've seen the Caterpillar!" the Mad Hatter said, sounding pleased. "I have been trying to get him to come for tea, but it's so difficult. He is so awfully small and it takes him a very long time to get anywhere. He doesn't much like to move at all. I've told him before, he should consider growing wings if walking is so difficult, but he hasn't taken me up on the idea yet."

"How terrible," Alice said. "Look, the Jabberwocky is on his way. When he comes, he should be able to let you out. He's missed you dearly. He really liked your hat, anyway. A lot more than he ever liked me."

"Now, if only you would bathe more often," the Hatter chided her. "He would like you fine without the hat if you could just do that."

"What's a Jabberwocky?" one of the men around the table asked.

"It's a dragon," the boy in the corner said, sounding amazed and having snapped out of his trance to be put in another one. Now it was one of amazement instead of horror. "He has a dragon that does whatever he asks and it breathes fire and it's *huge*."

There was a clamour above them as voices called out, yelling and screaming about fire. "And it sounds like he's arrived," Alice said, sounding more amused than anything else. "This should make things pretty interesting."

"Oh good!" the Mad Hatter said. "I have missed him so. But we will need to finish our business before we go. I still have to find the March Hare and the White King. They have both been shirking their duties for far too long and it's time for them to get back to work."

"Already taken care of," Alice said. "Once the Jabber-wocky gets here, just head to the kitchens. A friend of mine has found them and is keeping them there for you."

"Oh excellent!" the Mad Hatter said, looking positively delighted. "If you no longer need it, then, may I have my hat back?"

Alice removed the hat from her head and placed it back over his original one. She turned back to the hallway that lead down to the jail and called out, "*Ábedecian bealu gásric ælwiht hércyme!*"

She went over to the Jail Bird in the corner and tapped on his beak. He opened his eyes blearily, slowly focusing on Alice. It took him a moment until he realized she was prob-ably out of her cell and he snapped to attention, pointing his spear back down at her and got ready to call for backup.

She smiled at him and stepped out of reach of his spear. "Hello," she said pleasantly. "You probably want to get out of here. There's a dragon coming."

He stared at her blankly, his heart too long gone for him to be confused at such a statement. "Back into your cell," he said.

"I don't think so," Alice said, stepping back and to the other end of the hall.

A moment later, the Jabberwocky came bounding through the door and slammed hard into the bird as he failed to make the tight corner or fit properly into the small space.

She watched as the Jabberwocky shook and tried to make himself fit. He knocked out the wall holding the cell bars up and it toppled open, setting everyone free so long as they were willing to try and squeeze past the dragon in the way. On the Jabberwocky's other side, there was a hole where the Jail Bird had been knocked through the wall where anyone who wanted to could easily run out into the grounds and risk the guards.

"That is the ugliest dragon I have ever seen," the pirate said.

"That's not terribly polite," the Hatter said, welcoming the Jabberwocky with open arms. The Jabberwocky seemed to like him well enough, though he was back to disliking Alice again. He hissed at her, recognizing her now without the hat as the creature that got him out of the nice safe woods by her school and into the terrible lands of Wonderland.

"Come now," the Mad Hatter said, hopping on the Jabberwocky's back. "We have more to do than to correct everyone here on their poor manners today. Alice says they're in the kitchen. Let's go!"

The rest of the prisoners looked on as he made his escape before slowly getting out of there as well. They opted for the hole in the wall, the pirate leading the charge with a loud battle cry into the grounds of the castle. Alice watched as the rest followed, but the boy hung back, staring at Alice.

"What are you going to do?" he asked. "You could have

left whenever you wanted and you stayed. And you came back. Why are you still here?"

"I'm here to save someone," Alice said. "I owe it to a friend to bring her brother back home. It's my fault he's here in the first place."

"Lance?"

"Yes," Alice said, looking down at him.

"So what are you going to do?"

"Oh, cause a distraction," Alice said. "The Queen of Hearts would really like my heart. Or my head. I'm not really sure at this point, but she wants me to be her daughter sometimes and sometimes she wants me dead."

"Isn't the dragon going to be a big enough distraction?"

"Oh no," Alice said. "The dragon is the getaway car. I'll need to lead everyone off the dragon."

"That sounds crazy."

"Something I'm learning today," Alice said to him, feeling almost relaxed amongst all of this madness. "In Wonderland, if it sounds like a stupid and crazy idea, that's probably the thing you should do. Because that makes the most sense. Now, if you'll excuse me."

Alice turned around and walked into the kitchens, stopping in the doorway. The head start did enough, as the Jabberwocky had beaten her here and was already swatting people out of its way while they tried to continue with their work. The Red Knight was here, looking to take on the Jabberwocky while the Mad Hatter yelled at him about how rude it was to point knives and swords at unarmed creatures.

Not that the Jabberwocky really cared. It had already broken through the ceiling as it reeled back on his hind legs and took a swipe to knock him away. The Red Knight went flying, landing over at the far wall. Alice wondered how much punishment he could take. Him, and those cards who were trying to tackle the dragon and getting set on fire.

"Hey!" Alice yelled across the room, drawing the attention of more than a few pairs of eyes. "Didn't you say the Queen of Hearts was looking for me?"

Their objective changed instantly. The still-on-fire cards continued to burn as they went through the kitchen, taking boiling water off the burners to douse their flames and never looking away from Alice. The Red Knight was on his feet soon after, pushing past the kitchen staff to get to the door.

"Alice, the Queen of Hearts commands that you surrender yourself," the Red Knight said. "You will come with me."

"If you can catch me," Alice said, looking back through the kitchen. She spotted Mike already seated on the Jabberwocky, who looked like he was going to do something stupid like run across the room to rescue her instead of getting on the dragon. She smiled and waved at him before dashing past the door, hoping that the Mad Hatter would keep Mike on the Jabberwocky's back.

Alice stayed in the hall, waiting at the other side as they came. More people and cards filed in from somewhere else in the castle and she vanished again as they got close, appearing behind them all and smiling. "Over here!" she said, luring them away from the kitchens and the front doors that were actually large enough for the Jabberwocky to escape through. Not that they'd go that way given the Hatter was driving, but she hoped the Jabberwocky was taking care of their exit.

"Come on," she continued to taunt as she lured them further and further away. "Can't you catch one little girl? It can't be that hard to catch me. It's for your Queen, right? And you'd do anything for her. And I'm so small. You can't possibly let me slip through your grasp this easily. You must not be trying very hard."

She stepped and found herself treading on a white metal foot. She looked up and found the dead eyed White Knight from what felt like so long ago, his hand coming down and grabbing her by the arm when she tried to escape. The rest of the Queen's guard were on their way, advancing in the distance as the White Knight pulled her in.

"Okay, so one of you is trying," Alice said, squirming to get out of his grasp. He had both arms around her and pulled her in a bear hug, her feet leaving the floor. He held her tight and she couldn't wiggle her way out or move enough to get out of there.

"Hello again," she said, stopping her struggle and looking up at him. She needed to think quickly. "So good to see you again, sir. I have to say, though, you really are hurting me by holding me so tight. I'm afraid I am going to bruise quite terribly if you handle me like that. Did the Queen say that she wanted me to come to her all injured? She does want me as a princess, after all, and a princess must never be injured, you understand."

That seemed to be enough for him. His grasp on her loosened, though his expression didn't change. Alice tried to make herself as large as she could manage, regretting wearing clothes that were good for moving quickly. She did the best she could, pushing her arms against his like she was much larger, and managed to make him loosen his grip.

Alice suddenly brought her arms as tightly in as she could manage. She dropped out of his hold before he knew what was happening and fell to the ground as the Red Knight approached.

She landed on the grass outside the castle and didn't stay to see the trees on fire or any of the carnage that the Jabber-wocky had done to the maze or the rest of the grounds. The hedgehogs could be on fire and she wouldn't care, taking off in a run across Wonderland to get away from the castle.

Her ten second sprint brought her to the tea party where

everyone was dismounting. Mike looked visibly shaken by travelling on the dragon over Wonderland, his eyes darting around to the tea party and like he was trying to make sense of just what had happened. He spotted Alice, doubled over and looking like she'd just run a marathon.

"Alice!" he said, going over to her side. "How did you get here? We just flew and…"

"Oh Alice," the Mad Hatter said, sweeping in and leading Alice over to the table. "Such a daring rescue. Perhaps not the best of manners to yell like that at a knight. There are rules to be observed, mind, but you have always seemed a bit dim when it came to proper rules of conduct. But come, you must join us for tea. There's a celebration to be had, now that we have the March Hare and the White King returned to us! It was quite a good rescue I performed if I do say so myself."

"You performed?" Mike said.

Alice straightened up and stepped between the Hatter and Mike. "I'm afraid we have another engagement," Alice said quickly. "Perhaps another day and another occasion. You have an unbirthday soon, don't you?"

"Oh yes!" The Hatter said. "So nice of you to remember. I shall expect to see you on my unbirthday for tea, then."

Alice smiled and curtsied. "Until then, farewell," she said. She grabbed Mike, who was still staring at the scene and not sure what to make of it, and pulled him away from the Mad

Hatter's tea party. She didn't stop pulling on him until they were back on the path and well away from that distraction.

Mike brought them to a stop as soon as Alice let go of his arm. Alice was glad for it, needing to catch her breath. She took a seat on the rock, rubbing her arms with certainty that there was going to be a bruise on them from the knight holding her so tightly.

"Alice, what is going on?" Mike demanded.

"We're going to find a mirror," Alice said. "And then we're going to go back."

"What? That doesn't — that's not what I meant. What happened with all of this? Why do people here know you? Where did you find *a dragon?*"

Alice looked at her watch. They didn't have much time left, but she couldn't drag him to a mirror. "One moment," she said, standing up and walking away. She found a mirror surrounded by chipped paint in the White Rabbit's house, still unoccupied. It was a dressing mirror, a little heavy and awkward to carry, but she picked it up and walked back a few paces to appear again in the path in front of Mike, who was now slack jawed at watching Alice vanish and reappear.

"I will answer all of your questions," Alice said as Mike went in front of the mirror and stared into it. On the other side, it wasn't his reflection but Alice's room. "I don't have much time right now, though. My parents are going to come and check on me soon. I need you to go through and hide until they go to work and I will answer all of your questions."

Mike hesitated.

"Please," Alice said. "I know this whole thing was confusing and you have a lot of questions, but I really need to not get in any more trouble than I already am in. Please."

Reluctantly, Mike put his hand up to the mirror and it went through. He pulled his hand back and looked at Alice again for confirmation. When she nodded, looking annoyed that he wasn't moving any faster and like she might push him herself, he finally stepped through.

"One brother down," Alice muttered, following after him back into her room.

CHAPTER 4

Freaking Out

MIKE WAS BUSY getting back to his feet and staring around the room when Alice came through. She couldn't hear anything downstairs and worried that she was late. With Mike standing in the middle of the room, he was going to get caught and she had no idea how she was going to explain how he got there or what was going on.

"Hide!" she hissed at him and she pushed him into her washroom, much to his confusion, and shut the door behind him. She didn't have time to change, but she occasionally slept in this shirt, so it might be all right. She pulled her covers up higher with her shoes still on, just in time for the lock to click.

"Alice?" her mother asked as she walked in. "Alice, you really need to stop sleeping so much."

"Sorry Mom," she said, yawning and hoping she didn't have anything on her that might make it look like she'd been outside. She was careful not to let the blankets slip down to show she was dressed as she sat up.

Her mother went to the washroom and let herself in. Alice's breath caught in her throat, her mind blank with panic, but there was no one there. Her mother pulled out her purse and a tube of lipstick so she could fix her makeup in the mirror. Alice forced herself to stay sitting as her mother continued.

"I need to get to work, Alice," she said, finishing her makeup and throwing the tube back into her purse. "I'm running late. Ms. Miller is going to be late today, too. Have you been going over things for next year?"

"Yes, Mom," Alice said, letting out a breath as her mother exited the washroom and turned the light out. "Have a good day at work."

Alice stayed where she was, as still as she could manage until she heard the lock click on her door. She relaxed, though didn't move, waiting for the sound of the front door.

As soon as the heavy front door closed, she jumped out of bed and went to the washroom. "Mike?" she asked, looking around to try and see where he'd gone. The shower was empty and he wasn't on the ceiling, which had nowhere to hide on it anyway.

The cupboard swung open and Mike crawled out, knocking a bottle of her medication out with him. "You have so much explaining to do," he said, crawling out and picking up the bottle.

He looked at the label on it before putting it back and righting himself. He stretched, his back cracking before he turned to Alice. "Somehow, this all has something to do with you. Talk."

Alice hesitated. She owed him an explanation, but she wasn't used to talking about Wonderland, especially not to someone who was staring her down that accusingly. Adrianna had been nice about it, but Mike looked pissed off and she shrank against his accusing look.

"I… uh…" She hesitated, her mind going through the ways to make her not sound completely insane while she was explaining this. Maybe she could just tell him that he imagined the whole thing, like the doctors had all done with her. Except that wouldn't explain why he was here.

"You cannot be serious," he said, pushing past her into her room. "You got an ugly looking dragon into a castle and lured away a huge knight and a bunch of sentient playing cards on foot, then ran, *on foot*, to catch up to said dragon, then just vanish and reappear with a mirror and make a portal back home and *now* you're nervous?"

"I'm sorry."

"Where even was that?" he asked, his voice only getting louder. "There were talking playing cards and talking flowers and talking bugs and *everything* talked! And there were things growing on trees that shouldn't be growing on trees and I couldn't eat anything or else I'd shrink or grow or *something* weird would happen." He ran a hand through his hair and couldn't stop pacing back and forth across Alice's room.

Alice didn't remember ever having this much of a reaction to Wonderland. She got back the first time and was upset by how everyone kept saying she was rude when she was trying to be as polite as she could. Mike looked like he was going to have a breakdown now that he was back on this side of the mirror.

"I need some air," he said. Alice went to the window, throwing it open along with the curtains for him, but she turned around to find him turning the doorknob. "What the…" he muttered, pulling and pushing on the door harder.

"I'm grounded," Alice said. "I'm not allowed out."

Mike stared at her, dumbfounded.

Alice opened her bottom drawer and pulled out an apple. She was getting hungry and she had a feeling that was only going to get worse as time went on. "There's some snacks in the drawer," she said as he continued to look at her. "It's not much, but if you're hungry…"

"Thanks," he said, going over to take a look. Alice moved to her bed, taking off her shoes and watching as he started to eat.

Mike took a seat on the floor, leaning back against her

desk. Something seemed to occur to him. "Hey Alice?" he asked. "What's the date?"

"What?"

"The date," he said. "That was the first thing Evan asked that night too. What's the date?"

"July thirteenth," Alice said. "You were in Wonderland for a little over two weeks."

"Oh." It looked like someone had just told him that someone had died. She could see him thinking and ate her apple in silence as she let him try to come to terms with what happened. He was taking it all so much worse than she did, but she was also much younger and more willing to accept that it actually happened. He looked like he was struggling.

"So," he said after a while. "That place is called Wonderland."

"Yes," Alice said.

"And that all really happened." He looked up at Alice and she could see he really needed her to say yes.

Alice looked away, bringing her knees up to her chest and hugging them tight. "It's better if you pretend it didn't," she said. "Just forget it happened."

"*I rode on a dragon*," he said. "I am not forgetting that."

Alice stayed quiet. She didn't even know how she was going to get him home. She didn't know how to tell Adrianna she found one of her brothers. Now that he was out of

Wonderland, Alice didn't know what she was supposed to do with him. And now he was trying to deal with Wonderland happening and she didn't even know how to do that right. Whenever she came back, she didn't have anyone to show her what she was supposed to do. She tried to talk about it and ended up at the doctors over and over again.

"Everyone's probably worried that I've been gone this long," he said when Alice went quiet. "Dad's probably furious that I ran off. Matt and Ad... Mark are probably going nuts."

Alice let out a small groan, muttering quietly.

"What?"

"I haven't found them yet," she said, sinking her head into her knees.

"Found...?"

"Mark and Matt," Alice said. "You were the first one I found. I'm still looking for them."

"They're..."

"I'm sorry!" Alice said, looking up over her knees and hugging them close. She could feel the desperation well up in her. This was easier in Wonderland. Here, she felt like she needed to do things so differently. To explain and not explain and make sure they knew that she didn't believe it even though she did. She didn't know what she was doing anymore.

The words started pouring out of her, unbidden and nervous. "I don't know how Cat got back through, but he was mad at me because I wouldn't let him out of Wonderland so he threw you in. And he did something so I couldn't get back through to find you right away. And then you were caught by the Red Knight and you are so lucky that nothing happened, but I haven't found any sign of Mark or Matt yet so I don't know if they're even okay or where they are..."

"Hey, hey," Mike said, getting up and going over to Alice. Tears streamed down her face as she talked, but Mike tried to calm her down. "It's okay. You got me out, right? I'm sure they're fine. They're probably off at a tea party somewhere, right?"

Alice sniffed and wiped the tears away. "They could be in a lot of trouble," Alice said. "I thought you were all together."

Mike looked hesitant. "I didn't even know they were in there," he said. "Hey, is there any way I can get in touch with my parents? Can I use your phone?"

"I don't have a phone."

"What?"

"I'm not allowed to have a phone," Alice said. "I'm sorry."

"A computer?" he asked. "If I can get online, I can probably get in touch with someone. What time is it?"

"Eight in the morning," Alice said.

"And you're on the west coast, right? In a couple hours, someone will be awake and I can get in touch with them," he said. He looked over at her desk and his face fell a little. "You don't…"

"I think I can get Lori's," Alice said. "It's still in her room. Hang on."

Alice got up and walked a few steps, appearing in Lori's room. It was dark, but she could still make out enough from the light streaming through the curtains. She picked up the computer on her desk, unplugging it from the wall and taking the cord and everything else that was attached to it with her. She wasn't sure which things he was going to need to use, so she just took it all with her back to her room.

"Is this okay?" Alice asked, handing him the mess of cables and laptop.

"That is ancient," he said, taking it from her and picking apart the cables and cords to get to the computer. He flipped it open and turned it on, grateful for the full battery, and ignored the rest of the cords for a bit. Alice took her seat against the bed and watched as he seemed to calm down from the panic from before and went to look over the computer.

"Can you get in touch with your family?" Alice asked after he started getting to work on it.

Mike shook his head. "I need to figure out the password. And then probably the wifi password. It's going to take me a bit, but I should be online soon enough."

He didn't seem worried about Wonderland anymore, at

least. He wasn't angry or demanding to know what happened anymore. Now Alice wanted to know everything that happened to him, if only so that she might get some clue about what happened to his brothers and give her a new place to look. She sat with her back against her bed and brought her knees up to her chest. "What happened after you got into Wonderland?"

He didn't look like he wanted to talk about it. He wanted answers, but Alice was not in any sort of shape right now to handle any questions and he shook his head. With his fingers moving across the keys, he took a deep breath and tried to think back to the beginning.

"So I remember that Cat walked out of a mirror out of nowhere and then falling. I landed in some weird patch of these really depressed flowers that wouldn't stop talking about how they weren't pretty anymore and fishing for compliments. And then going on about how I was a really crappy flower. It was weird, but at least you can walk away from flowers."

"I had a feeling those flowers were going to be annoying," Alice said with a sad laugh.

"Warn me next time." He smiled at her and Alice tried to return it. "It wasn't just them, though. It was everything in the place. There was a depressed... he said he was a Mock Turtle, but that thing was not like any turtle I'd ever seen, who was sad about a Gryphon being taken to the Queen. And there was this palace that had been completely destroyed except for one guy who kept adding pepper to a soup that wasn't even cooking. He kept saying that he had to fulfill his duty to some Duchess, but there wasn't even anyone else there. The whole place was destroyed except for this one guy and he's still making soup."

"That's just how Wonderland is," Alice told him. She yawned. She was getting tired.

"A few people said something about how I was as rude as a girl that came there once, but I didn't know what they meant. But I kept hearing about these people going missing, or animals I guess? They kept saying that people were being followed when they left and there were people in the forest. They said to stay on the path because if I was trying to hide, they would look off the path for me, and they were always looking for people who were hiding from them. That place made no sense."

He shook his head and kept typing in passwords. He looked up to Alice to see her still hiding behind her knees as he talked. He picked up the laptop and sat next to her, with his back to the bed and leaning forward to try password after password without success. "Do you know her computer password?"

"Um... Dinah one two five?"

Mike tried it and the computer started up. "Awesome," he

said. "So after I kept on the path for a while, there's these playing cards. Which, weird. But at this point, I didn't even care. Well, I didn't care until they started pointing their weapons at me and trying to make me come with them. Do you know the wifi password? Or your router brand?"

Alice yawned. "No, sorry."

Mike didn't stop typing. "So I started running. I thought I lost them and I was getting kind of thirsty, so I stopped and I see this little bottle that I thought was water that said *Drink Me*. So I did, which probably wasn't the smartest thing I've ever done. They don't see me anymore because I'm less than a foot tall and wandering through the forest. I'm safe, I guess, but I'm freaking out and then I find a little cake that says *Eat Me* on it. And I figure, I'm screwed anyway, so I eat the whole thing and suddenly, size of a house. I drank, like, a drop of the water again and manage to get back to normal, but the Red Knight already found me. I run, but he's fast. I didn't stand a chance.

"While he's hauling me off, we run into the Mad Hatter. He's got a few people with him and decides to ask to hitch a ride to the castle. I have no idea if the guy was serious, but I'm trying to tell him to run and he's trying to make the case that you shouldn't kidnap people who don't want to be kidnapped. Apparently he's on some most wanted list or something because he gets brought in with everyone else and me.

"Once we're thrown in the dungeons, I start to hear about a little more of what's been going on. There's an evil Queen who's going around stealing people's hearts and making people into these mindless drones. The Mad Hatter told me that if I really didn't want my heart taken, then I would just have to pretend like I never had one in the first place. He walked us through what it meant to have no heart in Wonderland.

"He also told me about a lot of the other stuff that was going on. He kept trying to get people together to storm the castle and get the White King and the March Hare. Apparently the White King was supposed to be leading some counter effort against the Queen of Hearts or something. He said that they tried to give the Queen a girl as her new daughter as an exchange for the King and the Hare, but the girl revolted and it turned out poorly. Seemed like he knew her from somewhere before, but I guess that was you, right?"

Alice let out a little grunt and Mike laughed, continuing to try and crack the password.

"He had some food, though. He fed us and made a tea party out of bricks. I don't really know how he did that. I just kind of turned around after a few minutes and there's a whole replica tea party there, but every time we ran out of food, he replaced it with bricks. And there wasn't much food to start with.

"So when they came for me, they brought three of us to

the Queen of Hearts. I did my best to go mechanical, but the other guys seemed to have something to prove. They let me go and the Queen just told me to go down to the kitchens and yelled at the other guards there to not bring her any more people without hearts. The other guys, though. I heard them as I was leaving. I don't know what happened, but I am going to hear that in my nightmares.

"And then I was in the kitchens until you showed up. God, no one is going to believe me when I tell them any of this, are they, Alice?"

Alice didn't respond.

"Alice?"

Mike looked over to see Alice slumped into her knees and arms, fast asleep. He brought one of the light blankets down off her bed and draped it around her before looking back at the computer. Answers would come later. First, he needed to get in touch with home again.

CHAPTER 5

Escape from Alice's Room

"I CAN'T JUST *not* say anything. She has to—"

Alice blinked slowly awake, curious about the sounds that didn't come from her dreamless sleep. She looked around to see she'd fallen asleep next to her bed, but someone had put a blanket over her anyway.

"Yeah, but—"

Mike was by her feet, his head sticking up from the corner of her bed. The laptop was open on his lap and something moved on the screen that he was talking to.

"Don't you see anything wrong with this?"

Alice got up and crawled over to see what he was doing. He had a headset on, pulled from the mess of cords, and the mic in front of his face as he was talking into the screen. On it, she saw a box with someone who she thought was probably Joe. She wasn't sure, since his black hair was now done up in large spikes and he looked like he was wearing more jewellery than she'd ever seen on him. And dark makeup. All around him were posters of people Alice could almost recognize.

"I can't just—"

Joe caught sight of her through the screen and waved. Mike looked over his shoulder at Alice and his hand hovered over the lid of the computer like he was about to slam it shut. He pulled his hand back and pulled the headset off instead. "Sleep well?" he asked.

Alice nodded. "I didn't know you could do this on a computer. Is that Joe?"

Mike looked back at the screen, grinning. He unplugged one of the cables. "Say hi."

"Hey Alice," Joe said. "How's your summer?"

Alice shrugged. "I'm grounded. Why are you wearing make up?"

"Because I like it."

"Looks cool."

"Thanks. Is Lance giving you any trouble?"

Alice was about to respond when she realized what he said. Joe was smirking, but Mike looked annoyed back at the screen. "No, he's all right," she said. "I don't know how to get him to you, though."

"I just texted Evan," he said. "Once he gets online, we'll figure out how to fly Lance back home."

"You guys are both *way* too okay with all of this," Mike said. "You aren't even going to ask what happened? Or, you know, where Adam and Matt are?"

Joe tensed, then relaxed back into his seat. "They'll turn up," Joe said as if it were an inevitability. "You showed up fine, right?"

"On the other side of the country," Mike said. "Two weeks later. Seriously, was no one even a little worried that I was missing?"

"Just Evan, but you know how he gets."

Mike stared back at the screen, frowning and shaking his head softly. Alice thought it was a little weird too, but didn't want to say anything in case it wasn't actually that weird to anyone else. Mike looked almost hurt and he opened his mouth to speak when Alice cut in.

"How's Adrianna? Is she there?"

"She's out with Dad and Claudia today," Joe said. "I'll tell her you said hi. Do you have a number so she can call you, actually? I'm surprised you didn't do that."

"She doesn't even have a phone," Mike said. "There is nothing to do in this room except read text books. It's no wonder Addie thinks you're so smart."

"Oh, there's Evan. I'll conference him in."

The screen changed to allow two boxes with people in them. Where Joe's room was plastered with posters and trinkets, Evan's was clean and precise. He looked a little flustered, but relieved to see Mike and Alice on screen.

"Ryan's in the middle of something downstairs," Evan said. "Could you give him a hand?"

"Sure," Joe said. Alice noticed black nail polish he wore as he got up. "You guys have fun. See you soon, Lance."

"Where have you *been*?" Evan demanded as soon as Joe was gone from the call. "It's been almost three weeks! I thought you guys had gone and gotten yourselves in even worse trouble and run off without telling any-one. And where's Adam and Matt? Tell me they're with you."

"Oh thank God," Mike said, the relief palatable and vis-ible on his face. "Joe was acting like disappearing was no big deal. What is going on with him?"

"Is that Alice?" Evan asked, noticing her for the first time. "Lance, where are you?"

"Should I be calling you Lance?" Alice asked.

"Don't you start," he said. "You still have explaining to do."

"You're at Alice's house, aren't you?"

"Locked in her room," Mike agreed. "Because she's grounded and apparently that means her parents use the door that locks *from the outside!* Who does that?"

"That might make things tricky," he said. Evan started

typing something, the keys clicking loudly. "Where are Adam and Matt?"

"They..." Mike hesitated and his eyes drifted away from the screen. "They aren't here."

"Then where are they?"

"We don't know." Mike looked down and off to the side.

Evan stopped typing for a moment, then got right back to it. "Alice?" he asked. "They went to that place I was, right? With, what did you call it? The Bander-something?"

"The what?" Mike asked, his head turning to looked at Alice.

Alice shrunk under his gaze, but kept talking to Evan. "No," she said. "It's different. I mean, you know they're missing. Everyone knows they're gone, right?"

"And it sounds like no one cares that we were gone at all," Mike said.

"I'll get them back," Alice told him. "I just— I found Mi— um, Lance first. I still need to find Mark and Matt before I can get them back. I can find them, though. I just need a little more time."

"I still want to know what happened there," Evan said, not looking at the camera as the typing continued. "I remember going into the forest, I remember seeing that thing the first time, I remember when you showed up and tried to negotiate with it and I remember coming back. I know I was missing.

And I also know I have a whole bunch of generic feeling memories of what I did during the time I was missing shoved in there."

"Wait, what happened?" Mike asked, looking between Evan on the screen and Alice. "Did he fall into Wonderland too?"

"What's Wonderland?"

"*Shhh*!" Alice hissed, eyes wide as she looked around for anyone who might be listening. They were alone, but now she had two sets of eyes looking at her, both of them concerned and hesitant in a way that reminded her of her mother when she first started insisting that Wonderland was real. "Look, both of you should just forget about what happened. Just stay out of the forest and stay away from Cat and you will never have to deal with it ever again. Any of it."

"Cat?" Evan asked. "The purple haired guy? I thought he was gone. What's he got to do with any of this?"

"He walked out of a mirror and dropped me into the Twilight Zone," Mike said. "I'll tell you all about it when I get back."

"No!" Alice said. She didn't realize how fast she was breathing or how hard her heart was beating. "You can't tell anyone about any of this. Just forget about all of this and just go back to normal like it never happened. If anyone finds out, they'll think you're crazy. And my father can't find out I've been back there again. He can't find out I've even mentioned it. Please, you have to just forget about all of it."

"Okay," Mike said quickly. "It's okay. We won't say anything. We'll never mention any of this ever again. Not a word. Okay?"

"Okay," Alice said, trying to get her breathing under control again. "Nothing good ever comes from talking about it."

"I believe you," Mike said. He met her eyes and held them until her shoulders relaxed.

"Now that we have that settled," Evan said, his eyes now returning back to the camera to look at them on the other side of the screen, "I'll come by to pick you up tomorrow. You just need to figure out a way to get to the airport. I'm coming in on United, so be by those gates at three."

"But how do I get to the airport?" Mike asked. "I didn't exactly bring cash when I took a trip into the land that must not be named. And there's the small problem of being trapped inside this room and Alice's potentially crazy parents."

"They aren't crazy," Alice said.

"That's up to you," Evan said. "I'm sure you'll figure out some way to get out of there. You've gotten into a lot stranger places. Although this is the first time you've ever been caught in a girl's room unsupervised without her parents knowing about it. Play safe, you two. I'll see you tomorrow."

Evan disconnected and Mike closed the lid of the laptop. "So what happened with him, exactly?" he asked, turning to Alice. "I'm not leaving until you tell me."

"You can't leave anyway."

"So we have time." he said.

She let out a sigh. She didn't like it, but if she indulged him, then he might do what she said and stay quiet about everything else. She spoke, keeping her voice low and her eyes kept darting to the door, waiting for it to open. "You remember when you were trying to figure out why you did all that research on your brother and you didn't know why? Evan was missing from a little before spring break until he caught us in the classroom. There's a creature out in the woods called a Bandersnatch and people were just wandering into it. And Evan was one of the people."

"But now everyone's been set free from it and it's gone, right?"

Alice shook her head no. "I did it a favour to keep the unworthy people from trespassing. He doesn't like it when his food comes easily and wants people to come intentionally to make him deals instead, so I did something so that people wouldn't get too close. He let Evan go for doing that, but I still have to figure out how to get Sarah and everyone else out of there."

"Sarah?"

"She's still there so you don't remember her. She liked giving people makeovers and finding people dates."

"There's got to be a way to get them out, though. How many people does he have?"

"There is," Alice said, bringing her knees up to her chest again and sinking forward into them. She didn't want to think about the garden of people he'd collected already. "I made a bet. If I win, he lets everyone go. All I have to do is figure out how to make him go away before I get out of middle school, then I win."

"I feel like there's a but here."

"But if I lose, I end up part of his garden like everyone else."

Mike was quiet for a moment. "But you can do it, right?"

Alice didn't say anything. With trying to find everyone who had been lost in Wonderland, she hadn't thought about it. Now that dread was back and looming over her again. She tried to push it away, reminding herself of what she needed to do first.

"I need to find Mark and Matt first. Or Mark and Adam."

"Adam and Matt," Mike corrected.

"I need to find them and get them back first," Alice said. "If I lose the bet, then they're going to be trapped over there somewhere and they aren't going to have any way back. I need to get them out first."

"But you have a plan, right?"

"I'll think of something," Alice said, hugging her knees tighter to her chest. She knew the answer was somewhere in the brown book currently hidden away in her closet. If the book didn't work, then she didn't know what she'd do. She didn't want to think about it anymore and she was running out of things to talk about that weren't related to Wonderland somehow.

There was a rap on the door, followed by the sound of the lock unlocking. Alice let out a sigh of relief for the distraction, but Mike jumped away as the door opened, the laptop clattering to the ground.

Ms. Miller walked in, taking one look at the scene and closed the door behind her. She wore a knee length skirt and casual shirt today, her hair tied back and a large bag on her back as usual. With the door closed, she let her eyes drift from Alice to Mike, her eyes slowly crawling over him.

"I swear this isn't what it looks like!" Mike said quickly, scrambling to his feet, his back pressed against the window.

"Oh?" Ms. Miller asked. "And what does it look like?"

"We're just talking. That's it. I swear."

Ms. Miller kept her gaze on him, accusing as he shrunk under it. She dropped her bag with a thud to the ground and took a couple steps forward, Mike looking like he might just throw himself out the window.

Alice looked back and forth between the two of them, her body relaxing. Her knees went down until she was sitting cross legged, trying to figure out what exactly Mike thought any of this looked like. Whatever it was, Mike looked panicked about it. From the look on Ms. Miller's face, that was just what she was planning. Alice tried not to smile too much.

"You," Ms. Miller demanded, advancing on Mike. "Full name."

"Lance Michael Case."

"Alice," she said, turning to look down at Alice, who was very relaxed and smirking in amusement. "Who is this?"

"Friend from school," Alice said. "He's Adrianna's brother."

"One of the triplets, I take it," Ms. Miller said, turning her attention back on him.

Mike tried to straighten up as much as he could under her appraising eye. He squirmed and glanced out the window as he considered his options. He let his shoulders drop and Alice could tell he was already coming up with some explanation for all of this.

Just as he opened his mouth to explain Ms. Miller let out a laugh and held up her hand to silence him. "Calm down, kid, I know you weren't doing anything."

"What?"

Alice giggled at the look on his face. He didn't seem to know what to do with this information and dumbly let Ms.

Miller guide him over to sit at the desk. She turned him so that he was facing her. Alice watched as Ms. Miller unloaded a few more books onto the desk as she talked.

"I said I know you weren't doing anything," Ms. Miller said. "And because of that, I'm not even going to ask how you managed to get in when the door was locked or why Lori's computer is sitting over there on the floor. There are, in fact, a lot of questions here that I am required to ask and I'm just not going to bother with them because I'm happy Alice has someone other than me to talk to while she's locked in her room for three weeks. Because of something, if I remember correctly, you were involved in."

Mike started to say something, looking appropriately guilty, but Ms. Miller continued to talk.

"On the other hand, I realize that your family is located on the other side of the damn country. Given that you don't even look like you're old enough to drive a car, I'm guessing there are some extenuating circumstances here that I'm not going to get an answer out of Alice on."

Ms. Miller gave Alice a meaningful look, Alice looking away under her gaze. "He just kind of showed up this morning," Alice said. It wasn't really a lie. She turned back to look at her. "His brother's been looking for him, though, and he needs to get to the airport tomorrow to meet him so he can go home."

Ms. Miller smiled and nodded. "I'm guessing you were using the computer to get in touch with your family," Ms. Miller said, nodding to the computer. "Well, so long as you didn't go out into the hall to get it, no harm."

"Why not the hall?" Mike asked.

"The security cameras," Ms. Miller said. "Didn't Alice mention those?"

"You have security cameras *inside your house?*"

Alice shrugged. "Dad's really paranoid about security," Alice said. "There's one in the hall."

Mike's jaw hung open and he tried to find the words that wouldn't come. Ms. Miller just grinned to herself, going through the books in the top drawer and removing the first Harry Potter book. She put it back in her bag and replaced it with the next two in the series, both with very dull look-ing textbook covers. She checked the bottom drawer, finding that they had worked their way through half of the snacks already.

"We'll talk about how to break you out of here in a bit, Lance, but in the meantime, what do you want for lunch?"

"You are *way* too okay with all of this," Mike told her.

"I've been with Alice for a few years now," Ms. Miller said. "You learn to roll with things after a while."

"Chicken something today please?" Alice asked.

"Sure. You allergic to anything?"

Mike shook his head no and Ms. Miller let herself out, fiddling with the lock before going downstairs to clean and prepare lunch. Mike just stared after her and kept trying to put everything together in his head. Between Wonderland and everything that had just happened, he looked like his head was about to explode.

"Are you okay?" Alice asked once the silence became uncomfortable.

"Your life is so crazy," Mike said. Alice bristled at the word, but he didn't seem to notice. "This stuff with going to that other place through the mirror and all the crazy stuff that goes on over there. The getting locked in and everyone being so *okay* with that. And let's not forget the teleporting. Somehow the teleporting is the least weird thing about today."

"I don't teleport," Alice said, keeping her voice down. "People can't teleport. I just kind of... walk."

"You disappear from one place and reappear in another. That's teleporting. And I have seen you do it a lot today. And yesterday maybe? I don't know how long I was there or how the days worked, but you can definitely do it. How did you learn to teleport? That seems like an easy question. How did you figure out how to teleport?"

"Oh," Alice said, glancing at the door. Mike was being too loud, but she didn't know how to ask him to stop. "I learned to do that from a treacle tart."

"A…" Mike looked at her, but his mind seemed to have broken at this point. He kept blinking like it was going to make sense eventually, but it never did. "Okay. I think when I get home, I'll look up a recipe. Maybe I can do that too."

"Can we not talk about this anymore while Ms. Miller is here?" Alice asked. "She shouldn't know I've gone back either."

"Why not?" Mike asked. "She seems pretty cool about everything. Like, way too laid back."

Alice shook her head. "She can't know either," Alice said. "She's awesome and everything, but she can't know."

Mike seemed to take the hint and brought his volume down. "So who is she, anyway? A housekeeper or a nanny or something?"

"She's my tutor," Alice said shortly. She didn't want to add in any of the other reasons she was hired. "And she cleans some too. But since I'm grounded, she's only here to check in on me."

"And she locks the door on you when she leaves too."

"It's not locked," Alice said. "She just does that for the camera. She got in a lot of trouble once when she didn't and now she has to pretend to do it every time."

"Your life is nuts," Mike said, leaning back. "I guess I'm not getting any answers right now."

"Sorry."

"So can I ask why she's smuggling books in for you instead of something with wifi?"

"What?" Alice asked. Then she saw him looking through the top drawer with the books inside it. "Oh. I'm not usually allowed to read fiction unless it's in the curriculum, but Ms. Miller's started bringing me other books. We're trying not to let my father know so I don't get in trouble."

"So let me get this straight," he said. "You're grounded. You can't leave this room. You have no television, no computer, no phone, no anything electronic except the lights and the clock in here. Your shelf is filled with textbooks. Not even anything remotely fun like art or music or, like, French or something, but math and science and history textbooks. And now your tutor is sneaking you *Harry Potter* like it's illegal."

"That's about it," Ms. Miller said from the doorway. She handed Alice a large helping of a chicken fried rice, and a smaller one to Mike. "Her parents are a touch strict, but I don't see the harm in a little witchcraft in the readings. Especially not after *The Hobbit*. Oh, speaking of, did you want *Lord of the Rings*? It's the sequel to that one."

"Yes please," Alice said, separating her casserole into two parts and putting the second half in a Tupperware in her drawer.

"How anyone could call you rude is beyond me," Mike muttered, digging into the dish.

Alice glanced at Ms. Miller, who pretended not to hear that. Instead, she looked out over the lawn and frowned as she moved her finger over the glass in erratic patterns. She waited until they were almost done with their portions before finally saying anything.

"So we need to figure out how to smuggle you out of the house," Ms. Miller said, looking at Mike.

"What?"

"You need to meet your brother to head home tomorrow, right? Where are you meeting him and when?"

"Um, he said the airport at three. He's getting off at United."

"I can do that," Ms. Miller said. "And I have a spare room. You'll stay at my place tonight and I'll give you a lift to the airport tomorrow."

"Thank you," he said, the words almost a question. "You don't have to do that."

"I kind of do," Ms. Miller said. "Otherwise you're never getting home. How are you at climbing?"

Alice picked up the plan right away. Her eyes darted under her bed, then back to Ms. Miller, who nodded. "He can climb."

"Good," Ms. Miller said. "I need to do a few more things

downstairs and I'll be back in a couple hours. Lance, if you could be so kind, could you show Alice how to work a computer? She'll be getting one for school next semester and I don't want her to be too far behind in understanding how the internet works. Alice, you walk him through the plan."

"Okay," Mike said, not sure how to take any of it. Alice nodded beside him and Ms. Miller left, locking the door for real behind her.

"What the hell was that?" Mike asked as soon as he thought she was gone. "What plan? What is going on? God, I have not said that so many times in one day to anyone other than Matt before."

Alice went under her bed and got out the box, opening it to reveal the rope inside. "We had a plan," Alice said. "If something happened and I ever really needed to get out, I climb down the rope and get to the road and Ms. Miller would find me behind the oak tree at the end of the road."

Mike buried his face in his hands and then ran them through his hair. "I can't believe you have an escape plan for your own house. You could have run out of this being locked up thing at any time? Why are you still staying when your parents are *clearly insane*?"

"They're not insane," Alice told him, taking out the rope and starting to tie it to her bed. She tugged on the knot, finding the knot secure but her bed moved if she pulled on it too roughly. She looked between her bed and the window, deciding that it would be fine. She could move it back if it was pulled too far over. "They just want what's best for me. They just get forgetful sometimes and forget I'm here when they ground me, so this is just in case they leave me in here on my own for too long."

"Fine," he said. He didn't sound fine with it. "So what do I do after I climb out the window?"

Alice went to the window and pointed out the bushes on the side of the house that served as a divider between the lawn and the more forested parts of their property. "Stay by the bushes over there. There's a camera on the door, but if you stay on this side, then you'll be fine. These bushes go down into the creek. If you follow the creek uphill against the current, you should find the road pretty easily after that."

"I still can't believe you have an escape plan for your own house," he said. "I mean, we have one, but that's more if we pull something that pisses off the wrong people and we need to run from the cops or something. Then again, I can't believe anything that's happened today. I bet they'll put me in therapy for years if I tell anyone about any of this."

"That's why you shouldn't tell anyone," Alice said. "I mean it. Nothing good ever comes of it."

"You would know more than me," Mike said. "But you're going to tell me what the hell all that was one of these days,

Alice. I am never going to forget that and one of these days, I'm going to need to know what the hell happened. Wait, does Addie know about any of this stuff?"

"Don't tell her that you went!" Alice said. "She keeps wanting to go and I keep telling her it's too dangerous. She doesn't think it's that bad and she wants to see it."

"So she's known about it this whole time?"

"I didn't mean to tell her. I just kind of couldn't stop her from knowing after a while. I mean, look," Alice said, pointing at the mirror on the other side of the room. In the reflection was a faint hint of the White Rabbit's house over Alice's room. "It happens a lot and I'm trying to keep from doing it all the time, but after a while people start to notice."

"So you're magic?" Mike asked.

Alice shook her head. "I don't think so. Just really unfortunate and unlucky. If I were magic, this would all be a lot easier. I mean, if being magic is like it is in *Harry Potter* or *The Hobbit*. Everything was a lot easier for them."

"Harry nearly died in every single year of school," Mike said. "Like, multiple times. I remember the movies. And the books. I don't know if I'd call that easy."

"He also always knew what he had to do," Alice said. "Or, at least, he had Hermione to tell him. I don't even know how I'm going to find Mark and Matt yet. I don't know where to even start looking. I got lucky finding you, but I don't know if I can do that again. Everyone I know is either in jail, or they haven't seen anything, or they've had their heart taken and put into that room." Alice's eyes went wide at the memory.

"Alice?" Mike said. She looked at him and his eyes were on the mirror, the hearts in the reflection beating. Alice could almost hear them beating at her again, the hearts in the mirror still too close for comfort. It was like they were surrounding her again, threatening to pull her back in.

Mike couldn't stop looking at them either. Alice knew what was going through his mind, even if he didn't quite understand it yet. His heart was almost in there. She didn't know how to tell him that, yes, that's what probably happened to the people he left behind. Their hearts were stuck in that wall and would probably never get out because, as far as she knew, there was no way to put a heart back into a body.

"Sorry," she said, ripping her mind away from it. "Ms. Miller said you should show me how to use the internet, right?"

"Right," Mike said. He tore his eyes away from the mirror, now showing nothing of Wonderland in the reflection, and brought over Lori's computer. They spent the next hour staring at the screen as he tried to show her the basics of a computer and the internet. He skipped directly to the time wasting sites and the sites for research with the promise that he'd give her a hand further when they got back to school.

When Ms. Miller came back, Mike climbed out the window and off into the woods, leaving Alice to clean up the rope and hide it before her parents got home. Ms. Miller didn't say a word about that day for the rest of the summer.

CHAPTER 6

Back to School

ALICE WAS HAPPY to be going back to school. The rest of the summer had provided her with absolutely no leads as to the location of the rest of Adrianna's brothers. Instead, she had to start cutting back on her visits to Wonderland once she wasn't grounded because Ms. Miller came so much earlier and worried about how tired she was all the time.

Her trips to Wonderland were cut down to just the far more manageable weekends, but she worried that she was going to have to cut them back even more now that she was back in school. Not that she was that upset about it yet. While she felt bad that she couldn't spend as much time trying to find them anymore, she had absolutely no leads. Wherever Mark and Matt were, they hid themselves well. The Mad Hatter and everyone else she could think of eventually agreed to tell her if they saw anyone who looked like Mike — Lance? — in Wonderland anywhere.

The return to Lucena Academy had her going back to the same dorm room she left the year before, though she beat Adrianna in this time. Nothing about it had changed over the summer while they were gone except maybe the sheets, with the desks and beds still in place. Alice checked the counter under the sink in their washroom and found that their toiletries had'n been touched since they left.

Unpacking was quick, complete with new uniforms since her old ones were getting a little snug, and the books went back into their places. She put the large brown book back between the mattresses where she could get at it if she came up with anything she needed to research.

The only lead she had so far was trying the lure incantation to bring the boys out of whatever hiding spot they were in, but it hadn't worked yet. While she sometimes heard rustling, she never found anyone. She did find all new parts of Wonderland, including a lake that appeared to be made entirely of discarded sweets, but had found no traces of a couple boys whose manners did not measure up.

Once everything was in its place, Alice took out the last box. Her father gave it to her along with her school books, warning her that she was to only use it for school work and nothing trivial. Alice hadn't even opened it yet, but knew there was a computer in there. She should check to see if she even had anywhere to plug it in.

Alice was under her desk when the door opened. She hit her head, letting out a small cry of pain as she crawled back out and went to meet Adrianna in a hug.

"How was your vacation?" Alice asked, forgetting about the computer and sitting on her bed to watch as Adrianna unpacked. Unlike everyone else, both of them completely unpacked their bags and settled in on their first day back instead of going out into the crowds of people after dumping their stuff in their room to catch up. Alice was more content to wait until after the assembly to do all of that, provided that she didn't get lost this time.

Which she might, given that Cat was out there somewhere. This year, she came in with so much more to worry about than before. Last year, she just wanted to make friends. This year, she had to worry about finding Adrianna's lost brothers in Wonderland, winning her bet with the Bandersnatch so that she wouldn't disappear from everyone's memories to become a part of his garden, and try to make sure that Cat didn't do whatever it was he was planning. And she knew he had to be planning something.

"It was fun!" Adrianna said. "We went camping a few times, but it was mostly just hanging out at home. I heard you were grounded."

"Just for the first half," Alice told her. "It wasn't so bad, though. I managed to find Mike. Or Lance? What's his name, exactly?"

Adrianna laughed. "While we're at school, it's supposed to be Mike. They made us promise to call them Mike and Mark instead of Lance and Adam a few years ago because they thought it would be funny. I don't know if we have to do that again this year, though, because it's just Mike."

Alice's heart fell, instantly guilty about it, though Adrianna seemed very unconcerned about the whole thing. It was like how Joe was before, but Alice was still feeling very guilty about not having found them yet. She left so quickly last year, too.

"I'm sorry," Alice said. "I'll keep looking for them, but I haven't managed to find any leads yet. They have to be there somewhere, though. I mean, they weren't in the kitchens with Mike. Or the dungeons. So they're probably still out there somewhere and I just need to find them."

Alice hesitated in saying that they were fine. She really didn't know if they were or not at this point. They probably weren't harmed *physically* at least, but she had no idea what other things Wonderland might have cooked up for them. They could be buried neck deep somewhere and have some mole watching over them, waiting for them to blossom into a decent Wonderland resident for all she knew.

Maybe the two of them had even found one another and they were off surviving on their own. Alice really hoped that they wouldn't actually turn into Wonderland residents permanently if she took too long to find them. She had a horrible image with the two of them as Tweedle Dee and Tweedle Dum because she took too long.

"It's okay," Adrianna said, far too calm about the whole thing. "I'm sure you'll find them eventually."

"I don't even know where to start looking anymore," Alice said. She was expecting a very different reaction from Adrianna than that and pressed to get one. "I've looked all across Wonderland, but nothing yet. But I'm sure I'll find something soon. They have to be somewhere."

"And you already got Mike back!" Adrianna said. "So you'll find Adam and Matt eventually."

Alice watched her, but nothing else was wrong except how unconcerned she was about her missing brothers. She was worried when Alice fell into Wonderland before, at least. People noticed when she was gone, and even seemed to worry about her, so it wasn't just because they were in Wonderland. Since everyone remembered who they were, she knew it wasn't the Bandersnatch getting to them. Evan was worried too.

She needed to see if Mike was worried. Maybe Cat was doing something. If Cat could do anything like this.

They went down to the assembly and it was the same as last year. Alice looked around for the faces in the crowd, finding it strange to see Mike sitting there with only one other boy. She recognized Trevor, Matt's roommate, and wondered what was going on as they talked to one another. Maybe Mike was trying to explain why there was only one of him this year.

And Mike wasn't the only one getting questioned. As much as Alice felt a little bad about it for Adrianna, she was grateful that someone else noticed there was something missing in the Case family.

"So where's the other two?" Heather asked quietly. "I'm pretty sure there used to be three brothers."

"Oh," Adrianna said, sounding just as calm as before. "They didn't come home with us last year and they haven't come back yet."

"You mean they're missing?" Heather demanded. "What, did they run away or something? Where did they go?"

"We don't know," Adrianna said. "They'll turn up, though. Mike came back."

"Did he say where he went?"

"No," Adrianna said, pondering it. "I don't think I ever asked, though. But if he wanted to tell us, I'm sure he would have."

Heather stared at her for a moment before letting out an awkward laugh. "Good one," Heather said. "But really, where are they? They're just off pulling something, right? We don't have to worry about our dorm rooms filled with, like, shaving cream or something when we get back, do we?"

Adrianna laughed and Heather assumed it was a joke for now, but sooner or later she would realize that they were missing. Everyone would. Alice needed to track them down soon. Or, at the very least, she needed to figure out how to make Adrianna realize that her brothers being missing was something that she should be worried about.

Alice was out of places to look, but there was one thing that she was loathe to try. Still, she was out of options at this point. On stage they continued to talk about the school rules and tried to keep the performance light, but Alice wasn't paying attention. She wasn't paying attention to her friends anymore either.

She had to do it, she realized. It was her best chance to actually figure out where they were.

After the assembly got out, Alice slipped off to the washroom. Once she was sure she was alone, she stepped away and up to the hallway with the rooftop garden outside in the theatre. She listened, but there was no one else around for the moment.

Alice knew she wasn't alone. She could feel his smile on her more than his eyes, watching unseen as they had when he first found her here. Alice turned around.

Sitting in the window by the garden, a purple haired, purple eyed student smiled his far too wide smile at her. He drank from a Slurpee cup and relaxed easily in the windowsill with the light streaming over him. His eyes were on her and not leaving.

"So good to see you again, Alice. I see you managed to find one of them."

"Where are they, Cat?" she demanded. She didn't want to talk to him, but she knew this encounter had to happen. He would probably follow her like a shadow again all semester since he didn't seem to have anything better to do than just hang out on campus. If she was going to deal with that, at the very least she wanted some information.

"They are a great many options," he said, his smile only growing wider. "Could you be speaking of those boys of yours, the ones who are speaking to that pretty little roommate of yours right now? Perhaps the girl wondering where you have slipped off to."

"You know which people I mean, Cat," she said. She did not have time for this. If Heather was wondering where she'd run off to, she'd already been gone for too long. "The ones you threw into Wonderland. Where did they go?"

"Oh, Wonderland, I assume," he said. "As you've said, that is where they fell into. Their own fault, really. If they didn't want to fall, why would they have leaned so hard on the glass? It's not a very solid thing, glass. Always dropping people into other places."

"You should have asked before turning the mirror into a way into Wonderland," Alice countered. She really didn't want to deal with his double speak. "Very rude to be dropping people into Wonderland without asking them first."

Cat twitched, but his grin didn't falter. He looked impressed. "Ah, but they should have known that something that shows another world would lead you to one. It is amazing that they had not been thrown already into the world on the other side that they could see, where everything is precisely the same but where people walk the other way."

"That isn't how mirrors work."

"Isn't it?"

"No."

He chuckled and jumped up from his spot on the window sill, appearing behind Alice and draping an arm around her shoulder. "Perhaps that is how they should work," he purred into her ear. His breath was warm on her face and smelled of something she couldn't place.

"Perhaps you should just tell me where you sent them," Alice said, stepping out from under his arm and turning to face him. "I have looked all over Wonderland and they're nowhere. Where did you send them?"

He clicked his tongue in amusement and disapproval.

"Oh Alice, you think I have so much sway in where Wonderland seeks to take someone. I merely gave them the chance to explore. Where they went is their own concern. Did I tell you where to go when you went through before? No, you made that decision for yourself."

"You know—"

"You presume to know what I know," he continued. "The only ones who know where they are, the only ones who ever know quite where they are, are the boys themselves. And even then, so often we never quite know what we think we know, you know?" He smiled, a glimmer in his large purple eyes as he smiled back at her with that too wide grin. "Perhaps you would do better to ask them where they are."

"But I don't *know* where they are!" Alice said. "You sent them there!"

"I allowed them a new door to pass through," he said. "That door would take them where they would. I do not decide where they would pick to go, nor where Wonderland may choose to take them."

"Just tell me where in Wonderland you sent them."

"I merely opened the door," he said, slipping back from her and onto the window sill where it was warm. "I did not choose where they took it to."

"So you don't know where you sent them."

"The door leads only to Wonderland," Cat said. "There's

nowhere else that it leads. Where they have gone from there is not for me to decide, though I am sure they will have gone in the direction of their destination."

Alice's scream of frustration never made it out of her as someone made their way up the stairs. She wasn't sure if she was grateful or not to see Mike, but there he was, looking Cat over. "You again," Mike said. "I thought I heard something. What are you doing back here?"

He smiled that toothy grin at Mike, looking him over in turn and speaking to Alice. "My, this one doesn't appear to be happy to see me. Could it be that he did not enjoy his trip to Wonderland? A shame. Wonderland is so welcoming to visitors. Perhaps a little too welcoming."

He said the last line with an eyebrow raised as if he were trying to hint at something, but Alice didn't know what. "If you're not going to be useful, get out of here, Cat."

"The rudest child Wonderland had ever met," Cat said smiling. "You tried to find me, and now you seek to send me away. Perhaps you would do better to remember to mind your manners. There are folks who you would be able to better align yourself with if you did, and you will need allies in the coming times, Alice. No one wants to reward rudeness with favours."

Cat walked off, not vanishing until Mike turned his back

on him and looked to Alice. "Is he going to be following you around again this year?" Mike asked.

"I hope not," Alice said. "I found him this time. I was just trying to figure out where he sent Mark and Matt. I'm sorry I haven't figured out where they are or brought them back yet. I promise, I'm trying to find them."

"Take your time," he said, leading Alice back down the stairs. "I'm sure you'll find them one day."

"Weren't you the one freaking out about them being gone when I got you back?" Alice asked.

"Probably," Mike said. "But I figure, you'll figure it out. You found me, after all, so you'll probably be able to find them wherever they are."

"You're too calm about this," Alice said. She would need to ask Evan if this change in Mike happened since he got home. All of the Cases were too calm about having missing brothers. "But thanks for the confidence."

"Now if everyone else would stop freaking out about it," he said. "Seriously, it's like they think it's a huge deal that they're missing. People keep suggesting filing missing persons reports and all that. I mean, isn't that going a little far? They're just not here. It's not like they're all dead or something. They'll turn up just like I did. And they're probably fine."

"What if they had the same thing happen to them as happened to you?"

There was a moment of stricken panic across his face, but that faded away after a moment. Like Joe. "They'll be fine," he said. "They'll turn up."

That was weird. Alice was certain there was something going on here, but she didn't have a chance to ask about it. She needed to get back to everyone else who were probably wondering why her bathroom break had her running so far behind.

"I need to catch up to the others," Alice said.

"I still have questions for you," Mike said, grabbing her by the shoulder and stopping her. "You didn't answer any of them when I was there."

Alice stopped and thought for a moment. "I just got a new computer and I'll need a hand setting it up," she said. "Come by later tonight and we'll talk."

She ran forward and vanished around a corner.

CHAPTER 7

Catching Up

WHEN SHE REAPPEARED, Alice was in the main dorm room entrance and walking out into the mingling crowd of students. She managed to find Robert first, sitting on the couch in her line of sight, and went to join the rest of her friends.

"Alice!" Robert said. "About time! What took you so long?"

Alice smiled and took a seat next to him with everyone else, listening in more than joining as everyone went through what they did on their breaks.

Kevin was off in England with his parents, apparently on a trip for business. He still hadn't said what it was that his father did, but it involved a lot of travelling around and he was insistent on keeping his family with him.

Robert did some travelling as well, though didn't go nearly

so far. There was a summer cabin involved, with fishing and camping, much like Adrianna's vacation. The difference was Robert's older and younger brother were considerably less of a problem than Adrianna's family and no one ended up pranking anyone on their trip.

Amidst the stories of camping, Adrianna explained the family pranking rules. Apparently, the trouble streak wasn't contained to Mike, Mark, and Matt . They had a system, as Adrianna explained, where you were only allowed to prank up. No pulling anything on anyone younger than you, but you could work together with them.

Mike, Mark, and Matt had good teachers in the fine art of pulling a good prank that wouldn't get you in too much trouble. While theirs tended to be large scale and elaborate, the other brothers kept it smaller and personal. Adrianna did not participate in the games, instead only focusing on the clean up afterwards and making sure the people responsible got the credit they deserved.

Heather barely talked about her time off. They went up to visit her grandmother in New York, then she found a way to transition their conversation into comparing classes for the semester.

"At least I can use Wikipedia to research stuff this year," Robert said, sounding relieved. "Last year with actual books and pens and paper — I thought I was going to kill my wrist by the end of it."

"If you can get to Wikipedia," Kevin said. "They might have it blocked on the network."

"That's why I have you. You can get around all that stuff, right?"

"Why would I know how — Wait, what'll you do for me? Stop snoring? If you stop snoring, I'll get all the blocks on the network off your computer."

Alice sat back, listening as everyone started talking about computers and how much easier it was going to be to type instead of hand write this year. Adrianna seemed to know a lot about it, and they exchanged instant messenger names and ways to get in touch with one another late into the night after curfew.

"Do you have one, Alice?" Adrianna asked at the end.

"No," Alice said. "Sorry. Maybe I can get one this year? And an email."

"You don't have email? What about a phone?"

Alice shook her head. They looked at her like she'd just walked out of a cave covered in dirt. Alice shrunk away from their gaze. "Sorry," she said, not really sure what the big deal was. Everyone else turned to Adrianna with a mix of expressions on their faces.

"Show her our ways," Robert said. "And soon. I have a feeling everything's going to get a lot tougher this year and she actually knows all this stuff a lot better than I do."

Heather smacked him upside the head. "You are not bugging us at midnight to ask us about homework," she said. "And you aren't getting my number if you're just going to text me to beg for answers. Kev, can you keep a handle on him?"

"What, and have him try to get answers off *me* in the middle of the night? That happens already. If you can take some of it off my shoulders, that would be awesome. I might be able to actually sleep for once."

"Hey!" Robert said. "I'm not just going to be bugging everyone for answers. Jeez, is this what you guys think of me?"

"Yeah, pretty much," Heather told him, laughing.

Robert mocked offense. Alice was glad that someone else was the butt of the joke rather than her lack of understanding how any of this technology worked. Apparently this was a really big thing for everyone else, so she would have to catch up.

She mentally tried to go over everything that Mike had shown her back during summer. She knew he said something about Wikipedia. There was something about browsers or something like that, messengers, and things that she couldn't quite remember. Something Chan was a place to avoid, but she couldn't remember what that was. She wasn't sure what she needed to know that for, but there was a list of things he said she needed to stay away from.

She should have probably just kept Lori's computer in her room to try and familiarize herself with everything rather than trying desperately to remember it all now. She didn't know what she was getting into with any of this, or any of these things they said they were connecting with each other on.

They continued on through dinner, Alice just trying to follow along with all of these things they were talking about. Occasionally they would break something down for her, but eventually everyone gave up, with Adrianna promising to show Alice how everything worked. The fact that she was technologically Amish, as they put it, was so strange that they just didn't know how to deal with it.

When Alice got back up to her room, she finally took her computer out of the box under Adrianna's supervision. Adrianna walked her through what little setup was left, Adrianna noting that it looked like someone had already done most of it for her, before getting her email setup. She also instructed Alice to install a few things before they heard a knock at the door.

"And how's my favourite sister liking her first day back?"

Alice and Adrianna looked up from the computer to see Mike at the door, walking in and leaving it wide open. Adrianna smiled at him. "You mean your only sister?" Adrianna said. "Who are you sharing your room with now that Mark isn't here?"

"I got it to myself," Mike said. The apathy about their missing siblings worried Alice, but she let it drop for now. At least they acknowledged Mark and Matt were missing. "So, I hear Alice got her first computer and needed a hand."

"She doesn't know about *anything* yet," Adrianna said. "I've been showing her what I know."

"Well, at least it looks set up," Mike said, going to the desk and leaning over Alice's shoulder. "Move over, I want to check a few things.

Alice got out of her seat and let Mike take her place, his fingers moving over the keys. Windows opened so quickly that it looked like they were out of a movie. After a few minutes, Mike glanced at the door and leaned over. "So can I start getting some answers now?"

"What?" Alice asked, Adrianna even perking up at the question.

"I want to know what the hell happened in Wonderland," he said. "You've been there before and you said you were eventually going to answer my questions."

Alice became very still and her eyes shifting over to the door. Adrianna looked at both of them really confused, then followed Alice's eyes to the door. They weren't supposed to close it when there was a boy in there, even if he was family, and especially not when the dorm advisors were wandering around, but Alice could feel the apprehension welling up inside her.

"Right, you were over there, weren't you," Adrianna said, as if she were only just remembering. "Heather suggested I ask where you went when you disappeared and if you knew where Mark and Matt were. I forgot."

"You've both been doing that a lot," Alice said. "You should be a lot more concerned about the fact that two people in your family are missing. I've been worried about Lori and she's been gone for over a year now. I don't know if she'll turn up."

"But Matt and Mark will turn up," Mike said. "You're looking for them, too, so that should speed it up a bit. You have so much tracking software on here. I'm going to install a few things that should make your computer a little more private. Plus, a way around some of the school's blocks. But in exchange, you're actually answering my questions."

Alice looked back at the door, then back to Mike. "Fine," Alice said. "Just not so loud."

Mike nodded and kept his voice down. "First question. When they said that the Queen of Hearts was going to remove my heart, what did that mean? Literally? What does that do?"

Alice hesitated, glancing at the door that was still devoid of anyone walking past it. She was glad to be at the end of the hall sometimes. "The Queen of Hearts can remove hearts from people. Like, with her bare hands. When she does, they lose their madness and become these puppets that do whatever she says."

"Doesn't that kill you, though?"

"Not in Wonderland," Alice said. "At least, not with anyone *from* Wonderland. They've all lived, just without a heart."

"And where does she put all these hearts?"

"In her room," Alice said, trying to push that memory of the beating hearts out of her mind. "I already told you about this. Please ask about something else."

"Question two," he said. His eyes never left the screen. "How do you know the Mad Hatter and everyone else? They all seemed to know you for a while."

Alice looked back to Adrianna. She really didn't want to talk about it. "I met them a while back," Alice said eventually. "When I was little."

"Little?"

She looked pleadingly at Adrianna. She didn't want to tell the story if she could help it. She didn't even speak the story to Adrianna before, her eyes going to the door once again.

"When Alice was younger, she went to Wonderland for the first time," Adrianna said. "Six? Six. And she fell down a rabbit hole, and ended up in Wonderland. She met the Mad Hatter while she was down there, as well as the March Hare, the White Rabbit, and a whole bunch of other people. In the end, the Queen of Hearts wanted her to play a game and, because she played right and was going to win, she tried to cut off Alice's head. And then she got back, but she's not really sure how that happened."

Alice finally went to close the door as Adrianna was talking, needing the movement and to physically distance herself from the story. She also didn't want to risk someone overhearing any of it. She hoped no one would come to check on them, or that if they did, Mike was quick enough to hide again.

"She tried to cut off your head?" Mike asked, looking back at her in shocked.

"Well, the King of Hearts would have stopped it," Alice said. She felt a bit better now and locked the door. "I found that out a lot later, though. But I didn't go back again for a really long time after that. I didn't really want to because everyone there kept telling me I was rude and it gets really annoying."

"I remember something about that," Mike said, rubbing the back of his neck. "I'm starting to think I got off pretty easy while I was there."

"What happened to you while you were there?" Adrianna asked, eyes wide and genuinely curious.

"I ended up getting caught by some Red Knight and brought to the dungeons in the castle. Then I managed to trick them into thinking I didn't have a heart at all and ended up working in the kitchens just salting and stirring water for a really long time. Then Alice showed up and I rode a dragon out of there."

"A dragon?" Adrianna asked, looking to Alice to confirm.

"The Jabberwocky," Alice told her, Adrianna's eyes lighting up.

"Oh, I remember him!"

"I thought you said you never brought Addie to Wonderland."

"The Jabberwocky was in the woods," Adrianna said. "Alice found it and we thought it was eating people, but it was really nice."

"Nice to *you*," Alice said. "I brought it over to Wonderland because I thought it was the one who took Evan and maybe returning him to Wonderland would fix things, but it wasn't the Jabberwocky at all that did it."

"My family is just getting dragged through all this Wonderland stuff because of you, aren't they?" Mike said. He laughed and went back to the computer.

Alice sank down on the ground, sitting by her bed and brought her knees into her chest. "I didn't mean to," she said. "I didn't want to go back at all or have any of this happen. But everything just kept happening and I don't know what I'm going to do. I'll get your brothers back, though. I just need to find them."

"It's okay, Alice," Mike said. "Really. It's a great story that I can absolutely never tell anyone, right?"

He smiled at her and she felt a little better about the whole thing as he went back to work on her computer. "Okay, moving on," he said. "Three, who the hell is this Cat guy?"

"He's the Cheshire Cat," Alice said, straightening up in her sitting spot and crossing her arms. There was a quiet fuming in her voice as she spoke. "He's from Wonderland and I thought I got him to go back, but he's back now. I don't know how he got through the mirror. I'm not really sure how he sent other people through either, but I am going to need to figure out how to make him stop."

"So why was he following you around last year?"

"He wanted me to do something for him," Alice said. "I said no and he wasn't very happy about it."

"Your life is crazy. Have I mentioned that?"

"Once or twice," Alice said. "I didn't ask for any of this to happen. It all just keeps happening, but I think once I get your brothers out of there, I can make it all stop. New stuff just needs to stop happening and old stuff needs to stop coming back."

"It's not really so bad," Adrianna said. "Last semester was pretty quiet. It was just when Cat was following you around that it was really bad. Last semester there was the Jabberwocky and the Jubjub birds and they were kind of fun."

"Because they liked you," Alice protested.

"The what birds?"

"The Jubjub birds," Adrianna said. "The ghost last year was really just a bunch of these birds that screamed instead of chirped. Once Alice figured out how to make them quiet, they weren't so bad. They looked kinda silly."

"Can I see those things?" Mike asked. "I can think of someone I'd like to throw one of those nightmare screaming birds at."

"We are not moving the Jubjub birds or going anywhere near them," Alice said, but no one was being serious anymore.

"That should do it for the computer," Mike said after a few last keystrokes. "Consider it thanks for the rescue and the explanation." With that, he left, leaving Adrianna to teach Alice all about the internet.

CHAPTER 8

Dreams and Adventure

BETWEEN SCHOOLWORK AND the crash course on the internet, Alice was glad to be spending time in Wonderland. It was a lot simpler and she didn't have to worry about people wondering how she never heard of things like Youtube before. At least she learned to stop telling people about these things she found because, apparently, everything she found had already been around for years.

Alice slipped away after curfew on Saturday night and began her search for Adrianna's brothers again, not sure whether the hunt was going to turn up anything at all. It was completely devoid of leads whenever she went, but with the watch on her wrist to make sure she wasn't gone too long, she started anyway.

Wonderland dropped her on a plain this time. The wide stretch of grass was something immediately strange to her.

Usually Wonderland gave her rooms or paths or hallways of some sort. There were places that she was supposed to go by following them, but now she got to wander around a great expanse of knee high grass without any real direction.

It was kind of nice. In her quest to find the boys, she had talked to far more of Wonderland's remaining residents than she wanted to. They all wanted her to find someone who was missing or fill a function that a missing person used to fill for them. She obliged in exchange for information, of which they usually had absolutely none. It was like Wonderland was trying to make some point while she was here.

There was certainly something strange going on, though. A few of them had stories of a strange person walking around. It wasn't the same strange person every time, near as she could tell, but they were robbing them of biscuits or demanding information or shelter very rudely. She was fairly certain even the thieves in Wonderland knew enough to do so politely. Well, politely for Wonderland.

She never let herself really ponder it before, instead focusing on getting the job done and listening to them complain. If they weren't talking about Mark or Matt, which they never were, she let the matter drop and went back to the path provided for her until the clock said it was time for her to go back.

Today, she just wandered through the plains, finding a small creek running through the middle of it. She stopped and took a seat by it, wondering why she hadn't encountered anyone yet. Usually she only made it a few steps before someone demanded that she be rude to them, but out here there was no one. It was strange and she was anxiously waiting for someone to say something.

No sooner had the thought crossed her mind when something rustled in the bushes. It was a quiet sound at first, but it got quickly louder. Alice didn't move from her seat on the edge of the creek and watched as a small grey rabbit in a vest stumbled out, tripping head over heels right into the water.

Alice went to help him scramble out of the creek. "Are you alright?" she asked, helping him back to his feet.

He shook his fur out, drenching Alice and chattering the whole while. "I never!" he said. "I was out for a stroll when this *madwoman*—"

An axe landed hard next to them, decorated with straps of leather and a couple feathers. The rabbit scrambled behind Alice's legs.

"Madwoman throwing axes at you?" Alice asked, looking around for some sign of something to come out of the grass.

"Didn't even do the decency of introducing herself before attempting to assault me!" he said. "The very nerve of her. Not that you've been much better, mind. You've offered protection, however, so I will accept a certain level of rudeness on your behalf."

"You haven't introduced yourself either," Alice said. Her eyes were still scanning the grass for some sign of someone in the underbrush, but nothing so far. "And as you intruded on me, I believe that requires that you make the initial introductions."

The rabbit hesitated. "Why I think you are quite correct," he said. Alice looked down at him in shock when something came storming out of the underbrush towards them. She glanced up as the rabbit cowered behind her legs. "Though I would conjecture that perhaps we might place manners on hold to deal with the more serious issue soon to be present."

That was the closest thing to an apology she had ever gotten from anyone in Wonderland. As far as Alice was concerned, this rabbit was her new best friend and whoever was throwing axes at him was not going to continue to do so for long.

A girl emerged from the bushes, axe in hand and looking more than a little wild. She was dressed all in tan and beads, her straight black hair loose around her shoulders and lines drawn on her face in red. Her dark skin looked like it got that way from being in the sun all day. The look in her eyes was deadly, and she looked back to the rabbit cowering behind Alice and then up to her, then back down to the squirming rabbit again.

"Move," she said.

Alice dipped into a curtsy. "Hello, my name is Alice."

"I don't care about your name," the girl spat at her. "I care that you hide my prize. I have been hunting that creature and will bring it back to my tribe."

"Hunting?" Alice asked. She hadn't thought that Wonderland even had hunters, much less that anyone hunted. Though, granted, they had to get their meat from somewhere. Alice had never found a cow that didn't talk back to her when she walked past it, even if the words were slow and insulting, though she supposed they must be around.

"My people are hungry," the other girl said, speaking slowly and stepping slowly around so that she could get closer to the rabbit. Alice could feel the rabbit shuffling around her legs to keep Alice between the two of them. "We have had no meat in several days. This may not be much, but it will feed my people."

"If you would stop attempting to kill me, I will fetch you a crumpet!" the rabbit yelled at her from behind Alice's legs. At the other girl's shocked look, he squeaked and went back to cowering. "If you like crumpets, of course."

Alice made a note that everyone in Wonderland was a lot nicer when you were attempting to kill them. At least, the rabbits were.

"No one is killing anyone," Alice said, hands out and keeping herself between the girl and the rabbit.

The other girl hesitated a moment before she let a crest-fallen look overwhelm her face. Her raised axe fell down to her side and she let out a very resigned sigh. "I shall not hunt you any longer," she said, though she was not happy about it. "You may continue to wander, long ears."

"Well... well good then!" the rabbit said. He took a long look at her, waiting for her to pick up her axe once more. When she didn't, he stepped back from Alice's legs and gave her pant leg a tug.

Alice bent down and he spoke in a low whisper. "I do believe if you convince her to keep her word, I shall owe you a great debt, Miss Alice," he said. "But only if I survive, so you best do a good job!"

The rabbit trotted away and Alice watched him go. As much as she wanted it, she found it strange to have anyone from Wonderland not tell her that she was rude. She wondered what sort of favour a rabbit could do for her and what it could possibly mean. She doubted she would get to choose what he did.

Getting the rabbit to take her place with the Bandersnatch crossed her mind for a moment.

The other girl had sunk to the ground when Alice turned back to her. The devastation on her face quickly steeled into determination as soon as she realized Alice was looking at her, but Alice could still see how lost she was. She wasn't from Wonderland. She was hunting sentient creatures, for one, and still appeared to have her heart. She said something about her tribe as well, meaning that there might be a whole lot of people who were stuck here with her. For now, though, there was one girl in front of Alice.

"I'm sorry," Alice offered, though she came no closer. Alice eyed the axe in the other girl's hand and the finger she ran over the blade.

"We do not eat anything that might speak back," she said, though she might have been speaking to anyone. "My father has said. I don't know that he is always right."

Alice looked at her, and then took a seat on the other side of the creek. She stayed quiet, studying her and trying to decide what she should do. It wasn't right to leave her, but she was also very possibly dangerous with those axes and Alice didn't want one of them to end up in her head. Or anywhere else. She sat by the one that was thrown at the rabbit earlier, though she didn't touch it. It might have killed someone before. Maybe a rabbit that didn't talk.

"You do not seem like the rest," she said finally, the other girl looking up to look at Alice. Alice shrank against her gaze, not sure how to take her appraising glare. Alice really hoped she wasn't going to be hunted yet.

"I'm not exactly from around here," Alice said.

"Do you also flee as the land turns to death?"

Alice opened her mouth to reply, but couldn't think of what that meant. The land that turned to death wasn't really what she would call anywhere in Wonderland. There were tragedies back home that she'd heard of now that she had the internet and knew there were countries with a lot of death, but the other girl didn't look like she was from any of them. This girl was Native American as near as Alice could figure. Maybe she meant what happened to the Natives.

"No," Alice said finally, slowly and trying to watch the other girl for her reaction. She didn't look too dangerous right now. "I'm Alice," she said again, leaning forward and offering her hand.

"I am called Tiger Lily," the other girl said, not taking the extended hand. She put her axe away and relaxed. "I am the princess of the Piccaninny tribe. My people are starving in this land and I have vowed not to return until I have found some bounty to bring back to my people."

Alice thought for a moment. "Does it have to be rabbit?" she asked.

"It must be food and it must be enough to feed my people," Tiger Lily said. "We have been unable to find anything to eat on these plains that does not speak back to us when we hunt it. My father believes that a creature that speaks would be unlucky to eat. The children once found treats that asked to be eaten, but that resulted in many great troubles."

"Was it a cake that said *Eat Me*?" Alice asked.

Tiger Lily snapped up to stare at her. "You have seen them as well," she said, her eyes suspicious of her again.

"If you drink a little of the bottle that says *Drink Me*, you can eventually get back to normal," Alice told her. She got up and went to the tall grass. "But if all you need is a little food for your people, I think I might be able to help."

Alice reached into the grass, thinking of the kitchens and all the food that was always being made there. She had no idea who ate any of it, or if anyone ate it. The table was made for several guests, but there was never anyone over since the Queen of Hearts tended to steal her guest's hearts. And yet, there was a busy kitchen always working on food. They probably wouldn't miss a couple of the things they had there.

She pulled out a platter with a large roast turkey on it, placing it on the ground next to her before reaching back in to grab the stuffing. "You just want to avoid eating anything with mushrooms," Alice said, continuing to pull out a potato dish. "The supplier for the mushrooms is a little—"

"How do you do that?" Tiger Lily demanded, already next to Alice. She parted the grass, but saw nothing of where the food was coming from. "There is nothing here. How do you make all of this appear from the grass?" Her eyes narrowed, stepping back cautiously again with her axe back in hand. "What manner of creature are you?"

Alice stopped at pulling out the corn, holding it up as if it could protect her from an axe to the face. "I'm just a girl," Alice said. "I want to help if you're starving. I know how maddening it can be in Wonderland. I just... I don't mean any harm. Really."

"This land," Tiger Lily said, relaxing her grip on the axe a little. "You call it Wonderland?"

"Everyone does," Alice said. Her eyes did not leave the axe. Tomahawk. That's what a throwing axe was called. And Tiger Lily not only knew how to use it, but hers also looked particularly sharp. "Ask the... well, I guess you could have asked the rabbit, but he's not here. We could call him back?"

"I do not want to speak to any of the creatures that wander this land," Tiger Lily said. "They have all been insufferable. They dare call me rude."

"They also do that to everyone," Alice said. "If anyone says that you remind them of another rude girl, they're talking about me. Can you please put down the tomahawk?"

Tiger Lily hesitated, then opted not to, instead pouncing on Alice. Alice hit the ground and struggled against her, but Tiger Lily knew what she was doing in pinning Alice down. She tied her hands behind her back. "You will return with me!" she said once Alice was tied sufficiently, which wasn't very well. "I shall present you to my tribe as one who will provide us with food. We shall never starve and you will serve me."

Tiger Lily turned to start gathering the food and Alice knew she had too much to carry on her own. On the one hand, Alice could just get out of here. On the other, Alice knew that she still had time. She did feel bad for Tiger Lily. Her people were hungry and new to Wonderland. No one ever had fun their first time in Wonderland, and she hadn't even warned her about the Queen of Hearts yet.

Alice let out a sigh and stepped out of the loose ropes, appearing beside Tiger Lily to help her gather the food. Tiger Lily jumped and nearly dropped the turkey. "What manner of witch are you?" she demanded.

"I'm not a witch," Alice insisted, picking up the vegetables and balancing the stuffing on Tiger Lily's plate. "I've just been to Wonderland long enough that I know that there's some stuff that you really want to avoid eating. This should all be fine, though. I think. Well, the Queen isn't going to let herself eat anything poisonous or dangerous, right, so it should be fine?"

"This is a queen's food?" Tiger Lily asked, still watching Alice suspiciously. Once the food was balanced, she took a moment to watch her before starting to walk across the field.

Alice fell in step beside her. "How did you come by a queen's food in such a place?"

"I ate something I shouldn't have last year," Alice said. "If you find food here, try not to eat it. And if someone hands you food, ask a lot of questions. Maybe get them to try it first, just in case. Or find a fridge tree. I think the fridge trees are usually pretty good about not killing you. Well, so long as you don't get a fridge dropped on you." Alice smiled at the memory.

"You speak of many strange things," Tiger Lily said. "You are certainly a kinder witch than I have ever met before."

"Thanks?" Alice wasn't sure if that was a compliment or not. Witches were supposed to be horrible, terrifying creatures that ate children, weren't they? That is, they were unless it was the more recent iteration from the *Harry Potter* novels, but something told her that Tiger Lily had probably never read those before.

"You will eat everything before I give it to my people." It was not a request, but Alice didn't mind.

"Of course," Alice said. "It's nice to have someone around here not telling me I'm rude all the time. Where did you say you came from? Not Wonderland, that's for sure."

Tiger Lily looked at her sideways and grinned. "You ask many questions," she said. "Perhaps a game before we reach my tribe."

"Is that a good idea?" Alice asked, looking at how much stuff they were carrying. "We might drop something."

"A race," Tiger Lily said. "If I beat you, you will tell me one of your secrets and if you beat me, I shall tell you one of mine."

"Okay," Alice said. She didn't really have any secrets to divulge to this girl. She didn't know enough about Alice to know what to ask and, while she was in Wonderland, Alice was an open book. Well, when she wasn't being told she was rude constantly. "A race to where?"

"To the green flower," Tiger Lily said. She ran immediately, Alice left behind to try and spot it. Tiger Lily was swift and had good eyes, running to the green flower far in the distance and nothing she was carrying looking like it was wavering. Even the gravy boat she balanced on her head looked like it was staying in place. Alice was going to drop everything if she ran.

The terms were only the first one to the flower, though. And she had questions for Tiger Lily. With a smile, Alice dropped down into the grass and took a seat where the grass would cover her, sitting right next to the flower. She looked down at her watch, trying to see how much time she had. Time jumped since the last check by almost an hour, so she hoped that Tiger Lily's tribe wasn't too far away.

Tiger Lily was happy when she first arrived at the flower,

thinking she had won. "Hi," Alice said from the ground, smiling up at her. "I think I beat you here."

"How did you travel so fast?" Tiger Lily asked. "I didn't see you pass me? You are faster than that boy! You have cheated."

Alice got to her feet and gathered the vegetables in her hands again. "You said that the first one to the flower would win," she said. "You didn't say anything about having to run the whole way. So, I get to ask you for a secret now, right?"

She smiled brightly, but Tiger Lily looked like she was ready to get her tomahawk out again. Alice avoided her eyes for a bit and let her walk ahead. Her pace was a bit too fast for Alice to keep up by walking, so she ended up zigzagging through the field, appearing and disappearing and reappearing behind her every few steps. Tiger Lily never looked back, but it seemed that she heard Alice's bizarre path and slowed down for her.

"You do not walk," Tiger Lily said. "You move with no noise sometimes and with great sound other times that would scare all the rabbits away. You move from one side to another and yet you claim not to be a witch. I do not know that I believe you, Alice of Wonderland."

"I'm not really *of* Wonderland," Alice said. "I actually live at school right now. A place called Lucena Academy. It's far away from here and I'll need to get back to it soon."

"I don't know that I should trust you, Alice of Wonderland."

Alice rolled her eyes, but let her continue calling her that. "I think I had a question that I was supposed to be asking you. One of your secrets, right?"

"I will choose which secret I will give you," Tiger Lily said, sounding a bit more apprehensive than she did before. "I will need to choose it carefully, for I do not know what you will do with it."

"I'm really not a witch, you know," Alice said. "And I'm helping you. You don't need to be so worried about me. Oh, but before I forget, you should be worried about the Queen of Hearts."

"Why would I have to fear a Queen of Hearts?" Tiger Lily asked. "I have defeated men from other tribes who command my hand. I am certain some soft queen from this world will be easy to defeat. This land looks soft, for all it is. It is not bountiful, but its people are fat and lazy."

"Probably because she's taken to ripping the hearts out of people's chests with her bare hands," Alice said, growing quieter.

"She is a strong queen, then," Tiger Lily said, impressed. "She has earned her right to rule."

Alice decided not to argue that with the girl who could throw tomahawks and kept more than a couple things on her belt that could kill Alice. They walked in quiet until they made it back to her camp, a small circle of teepees around a fire that burned low in the day. She wondered if they were worried about catching the grass around them on fire, but figured they probably knew what they were doing. They were probably significantly more experienced in setting things on fire than Alice was.

Stranger, it smelled like someone else must have come back with meat. There appeared to be something already in the fire as it was dying down, though the meat smell was masked by the smell of herbs that she didn't recognize. Maybe they over-seasoned it and that was why they were leaving it there to burn on the fire.

"I have returned," Tiger Lily announced to the camp. Alice looked around, finding that the people that she brought with her were doing poorly. It wasn't the hunger that Alice noticed. None of them actually seemed to be starving at all. Instead, she saw the injured.

Wonderland was not a place where injury was supposed to happen. Not as she understood it. It wasn't until the Queen of Hearts started taking hearts and suddenly it became a far more common occurrence that people were coming out of places with bandages after a close call with the cards or the Red Knight. But this was something different all together.

There were people with limbs missing, but the bandages

weren't quite soaked through. Each was tied off with a number of leaves and things that looked like they were supposed to be helping. The ends weren't bleeding anymore, at least, but they were also charred. No, not charred. It was something else, the black too pure and deep to be anything resulting from a burn.

Others were fine, if you could call it that. Their healing process needed less attention, but they kept staring off into space, reliving a horrible nightmare that they could not escape from. Alice could sympathize, remembering the looks on everyone's faces when they remembered the cry of the Jubjub bird. It was probably what she looked like sometimes too. They walked, but it was slow and aimless.

There was one man who stepped forward to greet her, looking down at the food she had brought back with her. "You have returned, my daughter," he said, though his face was grim. "You have decided to steal."

"I have not, father," she said, standing strong. "This one stole. I have captured her and taken what she has stolen as rightfully ours."

"Hi," Alice said from behind the potatoes. "My name is Alice. I hope this is enough for everyone, but you know, if you don't think about food then you never really get hungry in Wonderland. I don't think."

"We will make her eat everything first to make sure there

are no effects," the chief said. Alice was amazed at his head-dress, looking so large and regal while the rest of him looked just as large and clearly able to snap Alice's neck if he wanted to. Which he looked like he was considering at the moment. "What is this creature who has stolen this feast?"

"Alice of Wonderland," Tiger Lily said, leading them both over to a spot by the fire where she could put down all the food. "She speaks strangely, but not in riddles like the prey does."

The chief did not take his eyes off of her. Alice found her mind cycling through and trying to figure out just how Tiger Lily was a princess when her father wasn't the king. It was a tribe, so they wouldn't have princesses, would they? Not that she was about to argue with someone who had a tomahawk.

He stabbed into the turkey and ripped out a small piece and shoved it at Alice. "Prove to us that your stolen spoils will not harm us," he said.

Alice stumbled backwards and landed on the ground when he shoved it in her face and looked up at him. Her eyes caught on something behind him. A dark shape circling in the sky behind him. Her eyes locked on it as she tentatively reached out to grab the small chunk of turkey offered to her.

Whatever it was swept in and went right between Alice and the chief, taking the bit of meat off the knife as it flew away. There was laughter in the air and Alice scrambled out of the way, checking her watch. Time to go.

Whatever was flying around, he laughed and proceeded to steal a whole leg off of the turkey. With him distracting the chief, Alice vanished off to a mirror so she could get back to her dorm.

Even without finding the boys, she knew she stumbled onto something that she was going to need to keep an eye on.

Chapter 9

Extracurricular Activities

AFTER SLEEPING THROUGH most Sundays for a couple weeks, people were starting to notice. Alice wasn't really sure how to fix that, but Wonderland trips now left her feeling so tired. On the bright side, though, Cat hadn't been bothering her and she was falling into a good, steady routine for her classes. On the down side, her friends were starting to get bored and wanted to join the extracurriculars open to second years. Worse, they wanted her to join. As if she didn't have enough to do already.

"Well, I'm going for the play," Heather said. "Something arts is always good. But I should probably do something a little more science related too. And some community service stuff if I can find it. There's just not enough time to get everything done with homework if I want to keep my GPA up. I should really look at something athletic too."

They were going through all of the options now that they'd come back from a whole day of collecting pamphlets and materials at the fair the school set up to showcase the various clubs. There was really far too much to do outside of school on this campus, which Alice figured was why her father liked it so much. It would keep her out of trouble. It might also keep her out of Wonderland if she tried anything with Heather's schedule.

"You planning on sleeping in there?" Robert asked, shuffling through the various flyers and trying to figure out what he wanted to do. "I don't know how you're planning on managing three clubs at once."

"Not just three," Heather said. "Three for now. I'll get a couple more next year, once I get used to this load. And a few more when we get to high school."

"Why?" Robert demanded.

"Do you know how much Universities look at your extracurricular these days?" Heather asked. "It's not enough to just be smart anymore. Good GPA, elected positions, leadership roles, helping the community, *and* you have to be really well rounded. I'm trying to get into Harvard, here."

"I should probably run for one of those council positions," Robert said, not sounding at all happy about it. He looked at the pamphlet that was looking for people in the younger years to help organize events with the council that promised experience and possible elected positions from within that might be useful.

"You know you don't have to do everything your parents tell you," Kevin said. "You have a brother that's going to take over for your dad anyway. You could do whatever you want."

"What does your dad do?" Alice asked.

"He's a senator," Robert said, sounding depressed. "He always wants us to get into politics too, but it's so boring. I don't care about any of it."

"Join the play with me, then," Heather said. "All of you guys could come with me. It'll be fun!"

"I don't know," Robert said. No one else was that excited about joining with her. Adrianna had a pass, having already joined choir last year, but Alice still needed to join something. It was required in second year to join at least one club, so she needed to think of something. Something easy that wouldn't take up too much time.

Something that wasn't a play.

"What are you kids doing?" Mike leaned in, looking over Adrianna's shoulder at the pamphlets. "Trying to figure out the required extra thing you have to do?"

"I'm trying to get them to join the play with me," Heather said. "They don't seem to want to do it. We're doing Sweeney Todd this year. It's going to be so much fun! And you guys could just do the chorus. That's pretty easy."

"No one wants to?" Mike asked, looking over and directly at Kevin. "I thought you'd be able to get at least one other person to do a musical with you. All that singing and dancing would be *never ending* fun."

Kevin glared back at Mike. "Really?" he asked. Mike played innocent, but Kevin's shoulders dropped and he let out a resigned sigh. "Fine, I'll try out with you," Kevin said, Heather letting out a little squeal of joy.

"Awesome! That's one. Now what can you do about the rest?" she asked Mike.

"I'm only good for one today, Heather," Mike said with a grin. "Technically I'm supposed to be recruiting. Gaming Club. Play games, make a game every year. Mostly just playing games. We really don't need anyone to do recruiting, so I just have to look busy."

"There's a Gaming Club?" Robert asked.

"We make the rookies make the game every year," Mike said, grinning. "Great experience. How are you with object oriented programming?"

"Uh...."

"You'll learn." Mike grinned and passed him a flyer. "See you in a week," he said before he went off to bother some-one else.

"Did... did I just join the Gaming Club?" Robert asked, looking down at the paper in front of him.

"I think so," Kevin said, taking the sheet from him and looking it over. "Well, you're done, at least."

Alice shuffled through the pages, trying to find something that she could do. Alice didn't know where to start. She'd never played a videogame in her life, so that was no good. Getting in front of people and talking sounded awful, so the play was not going to happen, nor was a student council position. She wasn't really good at anything here. Music was bad because Alice couldn't sing or play anything. She wasn't good at running or jumping or throwing things, so there wasn't much she could do athletically. Maybe she could just learn to play something like chess and join that.

There was one that she kept looking at as she went through the fliers on the table, Heather still picking up random ones and considering them as she sorted them into piles. It was a plain one with a crossed fist and sword on it, advertising something called "Combat Club" that insisted that it absolutely was not a fight club, so you could talk about it! Alice knew it was a reference, but she didn't know what to.

She picked up the pamphlet and went through it. Tiger Lily had the jump on her and hit her pretty hard into the ground. And the White Knight grabbed her, leaving her helpless if she didn't think and talk her way out of it. And Cat was back. It would be good to know how to wrangle out of his grasp as well if he decided to set his sights on her again.

"I don't know about that one, Alice," Robert said, looking at the pamphlet in her hand. "My brother said that the Combat Club guys play kind of rough. It's not really the kind of club for girls."

Heather froze and looked up from two pages in her hands, hands not moving as her head turned to glare at Robert. She held it there for a moment, Robert shifting in his seat before Heather turned to Alice. "Combat Club?" Heather asked, sounding much lighter than the atmosphere she created. "Sounds like fun. They do anything competitive?"

"Um," Alice said, looking through the sheet. "They've done competitions before. Mixed martial arts and fencing and some other stuff. It's not really clear how that works, though. I'm not really sure—"

"Awesome," Heather said. "You want to try out together?"

"Okay," Alice said, looking between her and Robert. She had missed something.

"Adrianna, you want to come too?"

"Sure!" Adrianna asked. "Just for support, though. I don't think I could actually hit someone."

"Oh, I think I could manage that," Heather said, looking sidelong at Robert again, who shifted away. Alice was definitely missing something, but Kevin was amused by the whole thing. "That should work as my sport requirement, though.

If they compete, that's awesome. If not, there's always basketball."

She put the sheets back down on the table and went back to the rest of it. "Still, we should probably make sure there's backups. I mean, if we can't do the stuff we want, we're going to need to find something else to replace it, right? I mean, we *have* to join at least one thing this year."

"And if we're you, we're joining ten," Kevin pointed out, looking at the small pile that she'd accumulated in front of her. "Don't you think maybe you should pull back a little on some of these?"

"Not if I'm getting into Harvard," Heather said.

"You're going to burn out."

"We'll see," she said, defiant and still looking through the pages. Adrianna didn't end up picking anything else, but Kevin offered to do Library Club with Alice if her plans for Combat Club fell through. The hope that she would be able to not constantly be bested when someone tried to grab her were so enticing that she started to get her hopes up. She didn't need to learn to punch anyone, but if she could learn to get out of it when someone grabbed her, that would be awesome.

Now all she needed was to find a few boys and rescue a certain blonde from obscurity and she would be done. Priorities, though. Heather was now going to hold her to signing up to the club and going for their welcome session for all the people interested. There would be no try out period for them, apparently, but they would run you through an introductory session to make sure you really did want to do it. There was also a permission slip for her parents in order for her to continue. She couldn't think of why her father would say no.

SATURDAY MORNING CAME a lot faster than Alice was expecting. Heather was at their door bright and early, smiling and completely ignoring the fact that they didn't have to be there for several hours, just to make sure Alice wasn't going to back out of it now.

"Well, you do tend to kind of disappear a lot," Heather said. "And I'm not walking in there alone, so I'm not letting you out of my sight."

Adrianna laughed, then went back to sleep, promising to show up for when they were put through their paces. Alice got changed into her gym clothes and joined Heather for a far too early breakfast, still yawning through her cereal and wishing that she could have gotten a few more hours sleep. Maybe right through the morning meeting.

Still, she was awake now and she tried to make the best of it. "You really think you're going to stick with this one if you make it through today?" Alice asked Heather. "You're signing up for so much stuff."

"It's this or basketball," Heather said, "and basketball isn't for another month."

"But aren't you also joining student council and a whole bunch of other stuff too? I mean, I saw your name down for the library club too, and you've been rehearsing for the play all week. The play auditions are tonight. How are you going to do all of them?"

"With really careful scheduling," Heather said, smiling. "But really, if this one works out then it's actually a lot better for me. Basketball is a bit too traditional and normal, plus I'd probably have to join something else in the spring once it was over. Plus, those practices are completely crazy when there's intramurals and games all over the place and going to other schools that would mean I miss meetings to something else."

"So this one doesn't have any mandatory competitions?" Alice asked, kind of glad about that. All she really wanted to know was how to get out of a hold when people grabbed her or held her somewhere she didn't want to be.

"You didn't do any research on these guys, did you?" Heather asked, laughing.

"Was I supposed to?"

"I guess not. I got curious though. Get this, it started out as, like, five different clubs. They couldn't get any funding.

None of them. One was karate, sword fighting, fencing, some other ones, all of them were trying to get some funding away from basketball and soccer and the other programs that get lots of money. Since they couldn't afford to go out and compete against other schools *and* get the equipment they needed, they ended up just competing against each other in this annual thing. After a while, they all got together and just became one big club and combined their funding. Inside the club, you can choose what you're good at and what you want to really work on. Once a year, they still have a competition and the winning specialties get to go out and compete against other schools in it. That way there's enough funding to go around. And if I pick my specialty right, then I can just go and compete and get a couple awards to add to my resume."

"A specialty?" Alice asked, her hopes falling. "This is starting to sound kind of complicated."

"It'll be fine," Heather said. "Just follow my lead and we'll both make it out of today awesome. Why did you want to join this club anyway?"

Alice hesitated. She couldn't really say anything about the Knights or Tiger Lily or anything else that happened in Wonderland. She was taking too long, so she went with the first thing that came to mind. "Well, after everything with Cat last year…" she started, stopping herself as soon as she realized she probably already said too much.

"Yeah, he was kind of nuts," Heather said. "What was his deal, anyway? He *really* seemed to have a thing for you."

"We have some history," Alice said, but proceeded to slowly take one long drink from her juice to keep from saying anything else. Heather didn't press and sat back, letting Alice continue to drink and not stopping her from her pursuit of the juice.

"We should head over," Heather said once they were done. "See what our competition is like. This is going to be great."

Alice smiled and followed after her, happy to be spending some time with Heather. Alice had no idea how she managed to split her focus between everything. Heather left her planner behind today, which was surprising. Alice had seen how complicated her system was and she assumed Heather needed it to keep track of everything. There were colours and post it notes and highlighters and all sorts of things that made it both beautiful and intimidating.

Alice was tired after a couple weeks of just balancing school and Wonderland. She wouldn't have time to sleep if she did as much as Heather, but somehow, Alice knew that if anyone could manage it, it would definitely be Heather. She was just really put together and ambitious. Maybe when all this was settled, Alice would try to be more like her.

If she beat the Bandersnatch.

The two of them arrived just in time for both of them

to be very happy they had one another. There were a lot of boys from their year and older who all looked like they were significantly bigger than the two of them. Alice looked around and determined that she was likely the smallest person there. Even Heather was a bit taller and much stronger than she was. There were a few other girls scattered around, but they looked like they were much better prepared for something called "Combat Club" than Alice was.

"Listen up!" An older boy walked into the middle of the room, followed by several other students, each looking like they were representative of something special in the club. Two of them held two different kinds of swords, there was one with just a stick and three others that had nothing on them at all except sweats and a look on their face like they were going to enjoy crushing some dreams.

Everyone quieted down and looked to the boy in the middle. Alice thought he looked like he stepped out of one of those action movies that Robert got her to watch, except bigger. He didn't smile, instead looking around the room like he was sizing everyone up.

"Welcome to Combat Club! My name is Terry and—"

He turned and pointed to three people near the back. "You three were asked to not come back last year. Out."

"You can't kick us out!"

"Oh can't I?" He raised an eyebrow as the room went quiet. "Tasha, want to take this?"

A girl that carried nothing on her stepped forward and smiled darkly. She tilted her head to one side until there was a very small crack that echoed in the silence.

"Justin?"

A boy from the side nodded, looking up from a tablet. "Already had their permission forms signed."

"You can't kick us out," one of the boys said, smirking and stepping forward.

Terry didn't falter. "I suppose we'll get right into the basic structure of meetings. We tend to start off each meeting with challenges. You can challenge anyone else who is present. Tasha will demonstrate."

"Come on, rich boy," Tasha said, waving the boy forward. "We have business."

He walked forward, cockiness and arrogance exuding from him with every step. Alice already didn't like the guy, who wasn't dressed for the day. He came in jeans and a baggy shirt, not even bothering to take off his shoes when he went to meet her. He kept his short cropped hair slicked back and barely looked at Tasha, his eyes back on his friends in the crowd and smirking the whole time.

"Now Jackson here is demonstrating what you shouldn't be wearing to practices," Terry said, not bothering to stop his commentating as one of the other people behind him stepped in to referee the match. Tasha took her spot on one side of the mat and Jackson was on the other, taking his hands out and balling them into fists in front of his face.

Where he was tense, Tasha looked calm. She looked him in the eyes, her hands loose in front of her. She held herself sideways and did not crouch as he did. She didn't need to, as she was shorter and looked much more confident than the boy smirking across from her.

"I'll show you what a man can do for you," Jackson said, laughing a little to himself.

"There will always be at least one referee to a match," Terry said. "Depending on the people involved, there may also be padding and proper equipment. Because it is a special occasion today, we will not be using any. Is that alright with both parties?"

"Let's get on with this," Jackson said.

Tasha nodded, the faint smile fading.

"Matches go a little something like this," Terry said, moving out of the way. The ref called the match to start and Jackson went in swinging. There was no control to what he was doing, just wild punches until he hopefully hit something.

Tasha didn't let a single one land. She barely needed to use her hands to block, just moving her body out of the way of his fists and staying just a little too far out of his reach. She looked like she was luring him, watching and waiting for the one slip up that she knew he would make.

And then it was over. Alice didn't even catch how it happened, but he was on the ground a second later, wind knocked out of him as he recoiled on his back, Tasha a few steps back and still at the ready. He let out a wheezing groan and curled over onto his side, clutching his stomach and trying to catch his breath between coughs.

Terry stood up at the end, starting the round of applause that erupted through the rest of the room. The ref stepped in to close the match, raising Tasha's hand in victory as the crowd cheered. No one could make out what she said over the applause, but Alice got the feeling that she had been waiting to do that.

"We usually do three rounds, but I think you all get the idea," Terry said.

"I can't believe some—"

Terry moved across the mat with an incredible amount of speed and stepped his foot down onto Jackson's chest, knocking the wind out of him again. He didn't break his composure, instead turning to the audience as if he'd done nothing and addressed them again. "Some of you may be wondering why we're picking on poor Jackson here," he said. "See, in Combat Club, we don't tolerate things like harassment. If you're here so that you can stare at our female members fighting with one another and make lewd comments, let Jackson here serve as a warning. It will not be tolerated."

The room was silent. Jackson's two friends didn't say anything.

"Good," Terry said, bright and happy once again. "Now for all you new folks, feel free to ask a lot of questions. After you take about ten laps. Let's go!"

The ten laps had a lot of people drop out on the spot. Some tried to make it and didn't make it that far. Alice was spurred on by Heather, who insisted that this was probably going to be fun if they got to actually beat up someone eventually. Heather mentioned specifically wanting to learn to do that to an older cousin of hers and Alice did her best to keep up.

Her best was actually a lot better than she thought it would be. Alice surprised herself by being able to keep up. She wasn't as fast as the actual members who ran with them, nowhere near in that good of shape, but she managed at least to keep up with Heather, who was taking it easy. They ended up racing the last lap, passing a few people who were looking tired. Heather won, but by not too much.

They broke up into smaller groups, those who were left, and went with each of the older students to different stations to learn about what sort of things they could specialize in and to get an idea of what everything was like. They got to pick up a practice sword and a wooden kendo sword. Terry sat out of the practice, saying that his specialty was a little too difficult for first timers. It wasn't until they got to Tasha that Alice thought she might really like it here.

Heather was up first, Tasha holding up her hands with thick pads on them and getting them to practice punching and fixing their form. "Good," Tasha told her. "You punch like you have an older brother."

"Cousin," she said. "You can teach me how to do that thing you did before, right?"

"Later," she said. "You think you'll hang around? A lot of first timers come in to check us out, but they don't come back to stay until a couple years later."

"Maybe," Heather said, her punch to the pad on Tasha's hand not quite as strong.

"Worried it's not going to get you into the school you want?" Tasha asked. "Look, you want a guaranteed way to get into something that will give you a medal, you focus in wrestling. But if you're doing as much as I think you're doing if you're trying to get into that school, then you're going to want some place to come for stress relief. And trust me; this place is awesome for stress relief."

Heather hesitated and backed away. "Maybe Alice should give this a go," she suggested. Alice stepped up, Tasha looking at her curiously for a moment before getting her to try a jab.

She corrected Alice's stance and form, making sure her thumb was outside of her fingers and tried to get her to throw herself into it a little more. Alice was a bit timid, but she gradually got it.

"You have a last name, Alice?" she asked.

"Liddell," Alice said, punctuating it with a punch to one of the pads on Tasha's hands. She was trying to picture something on there that made her mad, like Tasha said, but it was difficult thinking of anything. She was still tired from the running.

"Liddell?" Tasha asked, looking her over again. Alice pushed her headband back into place to keep her bangs from falling in her eyes. "You wouldn't happen to know a Loraine Liddell by chance, would you?"

Alice faltered. "She's my sister," Alice said. "Did you know her?"

"You could say that," she said, glowering around and looking for someone in the room to blame. When no one showed up, she opted to switch the subject. "Come on, picture someone you'd really like to punch in the face but you never really got the chance to. Parents. Teachers."

Alice's punches were lacklustre.

"Cat," Heather suggested.

"That's better!" Tasha said approvingly, Alice finally managing a good solid blow. "Just keep picturing this chick—"

"Guy," Heather corrected.

"— guy and keep going."

Practice wound down, Alice feeling completely exhausted, but happy too. It was more fun than she thought it would be, and having Heather there helped to make her feel a lot more comfortable. Heather was smiling at the end of it like she really wanted to keep going.

"You liked it too, right?" she asked Alice. "I think I can get my parents to sign for it."

"Me too," Alice said, smiling back. She would need to figure out how to send the permission form to her father in the first place. She didn't have an email address to email him, nor a phone number to fax him with, or even a fax machine to send it to him with. They said that there was a form to email to parents that they could give a digital signature on, but Alice still needed her father's email address.

They parted ways, Alice heading directly for the shower. Adrianna wasn't there, leaving Alice to change and do all the things she wanted to do on her own. Homework was done, but she found herself once again going to her computer and putting on Youtube videos for background noise as she went looking for her father's phone number.

When she found it, she went to the public phone to make the call. In her mind, she rehearsed what she had to say, but when she called, there was no one on the other end of the line, only an answering machine for the house. She ended up leaving a message, one that she hoped she sounded composed in, asking for her father's email address so that she could send him a permission form for the club she wanted to join. She offered her own, in case he wanted to email her instead.

After that was done, she went back up to her room and found herself looking through the brown book for the first time since she got back. She hadn't had a chance to before, now flipping through it to try and find something that she could use to try and make Mark and Matt a little easier to find. Things would fall into place soon enough, but she never quite forgot what she was supposed to be doing.

There was also the Bandersnatch to worry about, but Alice didn't bother with that for now. One thing at a time.

She felt the eyes over her shoulder and slammed the book shut, turning to look at the large, purple forest cat. The Cheshire Cat's grin was far too wide. The lines in his purple fur moved in lazy spirals. "After all that trouble, now you willingly try to drive yourself mad," he said, clearly amused. "Perhaps I should have left you alone the whole time if you were going to just read it anyway."

"What do you want?" she demanded.

"A little entertainment," he said, rolling on his back and flopping on her bed. "This world is so terribly boring. We must play a game again, Alice."

Alice got up and opened the drawer. Her hand and the book went into it, but came out between her mattresses where she carefully stashed the book away before retrieving her hand again. She left immediately, not looking to see if Cat stayed on her bed as she left, and went down to join everyone else for dinner.

She realized she was starving from all that exercise this morning. Heather and Kevin were conspicuously absent, so it was just her, Adrianna, and Robert.

"How did it go this morning?" Adrianna asked brightly. "I'm sorry I didn't make it. I fell asleep again." She sounded a little hoarse, like she did after singing for a while.

"It was fun!" Alice said. "I just need my father to sign a permission slip and I'll be able to join."

"Jackson always said the only girls who made it in were..." Robert hesitated, looking at Alice and coughed to cover up whatever it was he said they were. "But he's kind of a jerk, so maybe he's wrong."

"There was a guy named Jackson there today," she said. "A girl named Tasha beat him up right at the start of it all. It was fun."

"I bet it was my brother," he said. "I'm sorry for him. Dad keeps saying he's awesome, but he's such an asshole. Then again, dad's also kind of a jerk." Robert let out a deep, sad sigh. "I'm going to become a jerk when I grow up too, I bet."

"You won't," Alice said, trying to be comforting. "Heather will beat you up if you do."

"Thanks," he said, though he didn't seem too happy about it.

They finished up and headed over to watch the auditions. Adrianna revealed that she'd been helping Heather with her solo all afternoon while Alice had been avoiding the world. When they got there, it really showed how much work she'd put into it. Heather sang her piece wonderfully and with a good amount of power. She hardly even looked tired from all the running and punching and kicking and practice from this morning.

Kevin was there too, surprisingly. Or maybe not so much, since he was wrangled into it. For his audition, he sang a pop song they had never heard before. It was mostly in English, though Alice was pretty sure that some of it was definitely not. Robert said it was probably Korean, since Kevin did go to school in Korea before coming to Lucena Academy. It was slower and Kevin was surprisingly good.

They stayed to watch as the two of them paired up to act a scene out, which both managed to get through without a script in hand. They cheered their friends on for their performance and wondered how anyone couldn't cast them.

Alice, Adrianna, and Robert stuck around through the dancing section, which Heather did not keep up with very well. She stumbled through the movements. They cheered her on anyway, but Alice could tell Heather was still tired from that morning.

Kevin, on the other hand, was amazing. None of them really expected him to be good, but he was able to pick up the choreography easily and parrot it. He knew where his feet needed to go and where his arms needed to be. His wrists and ankles did not falter and he was one of the best there of any year.

Alice wondered what Mike had on him. Kevin didn't want to do this, even though it was clear that he knew what he was doing. More than that, he seemed to be enjoying himself. As much as Heather wanted the spot on the play, Alice thought that Kevin was better.

They headed back together, giving Kevin a hard time. Heather was probably the worst of them, though. "How come you didn't tell me you could dance?!" she demanded. "And sing!"

Kevin said nothing, blushing and keeping his head down the whole time. There was something he wasn't telling them, but Alice wasn't about to pressure it out of him. Robert, on the other hand, looked like he might attempt to strangle him in his sleep if he didn't tell them why he never mentioned that he was talented.

By the time they were back in their dorm, Alice was

exhausted. She still hadn't quite recovered from the deep-in-her-muscles fatigue from running all those laps and then hitting all the stations that morning.

"Maybe you should skip Wonderland this week," Adrianna suggested. "You look really tired. Maybe you can just try again next week and…"

When she turned around, Alice had already fallen asleep.

Chapter 10

Disappointments and Problems

It took a week before Alice finally got word back from her father. It was late Saturday evening and she was just getting ready to head into Wonderland when she got the notification of a new message. She quickly forwarded him the permission slip and headed to the mirror.

"It's Friday," Adrianna murmured from her bed. "Don't you just go to Wonderland on Saturdays?"

"I didn't go at all last week, so I'm going twice this time."

"Don't go for too long," Adrianna murmured from bed. "You're supposed to go in for library club by eleven tomorrow."

"Right," Alice said, checking her wrist. She forgot her watch. "Thanks," she said as she went back to her desk to get it and fasten it back in place. "I'll be back before too long. Promise."

Adrianna mumbled something and turned over, going back to sleep. Alice caught a flash of purple and a set of smiling teeth out of the corner of her eye as she turned back to the mirror and stepped through.

She came out deep in the forest. She didn't see a path anywhere, or even a bird to keep her company. Off in the distance, though, there was a crashing that was only getting farther away. From the sound and the sight in the distance of a tree bending out of a dark creatures way, Alice opted to travel in the opposite direction.

Alice made it all of three steps before she spotted the top hat, a different one than usual, making its way towards her. She would have tried to escape if he had not been waving at her from between the trees, having caught sight of her well before she saw him.

"Oh, Alice!" the Mad Hatter called. "Hello! How delightful to find you in such an odd place. Have you come to help me look as well?"

"Hello Hatter," Alice said, sure to greet him with a curtsy before she said anything more to address his actual question. Her Wonderland brain was only just starting to kick in. "I'm afraid I don't know what you're looking for."

"No need to be afraid, my dear," he said comfortingly. "It seems the Jabberwocky does not like my company as much as he used to, the silly thing. Keeps insisting on smashing my table and ruining my parties whenever I try to invite him to sit and join us. I think he might be a bit jealous now that the March Hare and the White King are joining us. One just can't compare to the company of a king, you understand. I fear the poor creature might feel somewhat inadequate. I keep trying to explain that his company is much more welcome these days, what with the King and the Hare being such terrible conversationalists."

Alice smiled and tried to look sympathetic. She would have run from his parties long ago if she'd been forced to attend them herself. "Oh my," she said. "Well, I suppose you can't really blame him for that. I mean, the White King is a king."

"I suppose you are right," the Mad Hatter said, looking resigned as he looked off into the forest.

Still, with the Jabberwocky loose in Wonderland and not under the care of the Mad Hatter, it was a little troubling. She was content to let him do what he wanted so long as he kept it from running loose. There wasn't much here in the way of birds to eat that wouldn't chatter away at him while he ate them.

"Come along, then," he said, waving Alice over as he walked back. "Might as well come back for a spot of tea before you so kindly go off to find the Jabberwocky and convince him to return."

"*I'm* going to find the Jabberwocky, now?" she asked, amused.

"Why, thank you for your delightful offer!" the Mad Hatter said. "So kind of you to search for the poor dear for me."

Alice knew she walked right into that one, but there was a lot more here than Jabberwocky vanishing. He was still somewhere. That he was now running away from the Mad Hatter bothered her. Before, he had been willing to go up close to him and only him. Even just wearing his hat was enough to gain the Jabberwocky's trust. She didn't like that he didn't have a master at the moment.

Looking at the Mad Hatter, she concluded it likely wasn't his fault. He behaved much the same way as he always did, walking over the branches in that way he did, weaving back and forth with a bit more nimble agility than it looked like he should have. He hadn't called her rude yet, which was a little odd, but he was also worried about his missing pet. He would call her rude by the end of the day.

They only went a short way before the trees parted, revealing the tea party. Alice really had no idea how he managed to have a tea party with him everywhere he went, but she also knew better than to try asking about it. He'd made a whole tea party out of bricks when he was in jail and made people drink the dust, after all.

Today, there were familiar faces around the table again,

though she was uneasy about all of them. The White King and the March Hare sat there, staring forward without blinking or moving. It was her fault in part that the White King had his heart removed in the first place, which made Alice uneasy around him more than those dead eyes. Now that she was closer, she could see their chests were a concave where their hearts should have been.

The last at the table glared at her from behind her hunting knife that she was busy sharpening. Tiger Lily was not so much happy to see her as she was curious. Alice hoped she wasn't curious about what Alice looked like carved up into a thousand little pieces. At least she looked calm this time, and like she was here as a guest rather than a prisoner. She had her feet up on another chair and she moved the dishes out of the way so she could put down her other weapons.

Of course, the Dormouse was asleep on a crumpet today. He was nibbling at it absently in his sleep and Alice wondered if maybe he was just really lazy instead of sleeping. She certainly would have liked to be lying on a large piece of popcorn and eating it right about now.

"Won't you join us, Alice?" the Hatter asked, holding out a chair. She was sure to take it from him and seat herself, though he made a noise of irritation when she did. "Have you met Tiger Lily? Delightful girl. A bit savage, though. Keeps putting her feet up on the chairs, but I haven't the heart to tell her how improper it is or to correct her."

Tiger Lily looked like she might grab one of her tomahawks and see how much of the Hatter's brain was concealed under that top hat. She held her tongue, however, and removed her feet from the chair. "I should take your tongue for such disrespect," she said.

"I should banish you from the table for your horrid manners!" the Hatter countered, turning away and going to tell the March Hare precisely all the things he thought he should do to ensure Tiger Lily knew how rude she was being to him at his own table.

Tiger Lily put down her whet stone and the knife. She leaned forward, her attention on Alice. "Alice of Wonderland," she said. "I see you have returned."

"Sorry," Alice said, shrinking under her gaze. "I told you before that I needed to get back to school soon."

"You did," Tiger Lily said. "You were lucky to have escaped so easily. The next time it will not be so easy."

Alice shrunk away from her, but tried to keep her posture under the Mad Hatter's eye. "I hoped there wouldn't be a next time," Alice said. This was, hopefully, a place where they were in a truce rather than at odds. "I mean, I was only trying to help. It's not like I was throwing an axe at you or anything."

"I do not trust you, Alice of Wonderland," she said. "You

offer gifts and have yet to ask a reward. No gifts can come at no cost when they are from a witch."

"Why Alice!" the Mad Hatter exclaimed, looking positively shocked. "You became a witch?"

"I'm not a witch!" Alice snapped. "Do I really look like a witch to you?"

"Your wickedness has not twisted your face yet," Tiger Lily conceded. "Not by much."

Alice glared at her, but held her tongue. She was used to the Mad Hatter making fun of her or telling her how improper she was, but now it was coming from someone who wasn't even from Wonderland. She wondered if she should just go home now.

"If I ask you for a favour, would you trust me?" Alice asked, an idea springing to her mind. "Because I've been looking—"

"Oh tut!" the Mad Hatter said. "No talk of business! This is meant to be a party!"

Tiger Lily let out a derisive noise and sat back in her seat, knife back in hand.

Alice looked around the table to find that no one was particularly happy. Even the Mad Hatter was busy gazing out into the forest every few moments, wringing his hands and hoping for the Jabberwocky to come bounding through to join them again. Alice hoped it had the sense to stay away until after she was gone. And that it would come back to the Mad Hatter. She really didn't want the Jabberwocky roaming free.

The Mad Hatter was looking at her. She didn't want to say anything to him at the moment, so instead went around the table and saw that there was precisely no one she wanted to talk to instead. Either the lifeless eyes or the potentially life taking knife waited for her and she wasn't fond of those options.

"So Dormouse," she said, going to the last refuge. The mouse might not make much conversation, what with the snoring, but it was still better than talking to the other options. "How have you liked having everyone back around the table?"

"Huh?" He opened a bleary eye, then the other one, looking up at Alice. "I'm awake. Just resting my eyes. What's that about people being back?"

"I meant mostly the March Hare. Though it's nice to have a king dining with us," she added quickly upon seeing the Mad Hatter's outrage in silent pantomime out of the corner of her eye. "Fantastic to have royalty with us, really, but I always thought that the March Hare was a bit of an old friend of yours."

"Oh, him," the Dormouse said, sounding unimpressed. "I've learned that people are quite dull when the heart of them is gone. And don't you start again," he said, his nose twitching in the direction of the Mad Hatter behind him. "Their manners may be impeccable, but they are not as they were.

I would prefer the sound of bickering to such silence. They have not brought anything to this party. I daresay they have brought less than the girl who threatened to skin me. At least she brought a little excitement."

"Excitement that was inappropriate for the occasion! She is lucky she had an offer or I would have thrown her out of the party!"

"Offer?" Alice asked. It was not her turn to speak, she realized, but the Mad Hatter was too flustered to reprimand her for it right now.

"Why, she is here to help find The Jabberwocky!" The Mad Hatter said. "Strange as she is, she seems like she should be able to track him down. Why, I saw her almost catch a field mouse!"

Alice looked at her and tried not to feel pity. The land was not made for hunting or any of the things the weapons in front of her were made for. Wonderland was silly and mad. There was food that grew on trees and food that simply appeared. Her people would need to give up the hunt here, for there was no bounty.

"If your people need more food I can—"

"I will owe no more favours to a witch." Tiger Lily glared at her over her knife.

"Don't mind her, dear. Worse manners than you. And she claims to be some princess from a far off land. If they are all like her, I should wonder why anyone would ever visit. Just awful."

"I am beginning to forget why I am offering my aid."

"You asked that I show you the plants," the Mad Hatter said very matter of factually. "You wished to know what all of them did and would assist me should I assist you."

"Be sure to warn her about the treacle," Alice said, a wry grin across her face.

The Mad Hatter laughed. "Oh, Alice. Treacle is not a plant." He turned to Tiger Lily, but did not lower his voice when he spoke to her. "Nice girl, Alice. But not terribly bright."

Tiger Lily took great joy in that, but Alice managed to keep from defending herself. "So if Tiger Lily is looking for the Jabberwocky, then I suppose you will not need me to assist in the search." Alice cheered up at the thought.

"Nonsense," he said. "I do believe that they say two heads are far superior to one. And besides, he knows you, Alice. He will need a familiar face there when he is found. Oh, he is probably so frightened, being all alone like he is. Poor dear, he will need plenty of crumpets when he returns."

"I'm sure Tiger Lily knows how to comfort a dragon," Alice said as she looked hopefully to Tiger Lily, but Tiger Lily stayed quiet. Apparently she was willing to work with a witch if it meant the witch was going to suffer a little in the mean-time.

"Ah, but you have far more experience, don't be so modest." He smiled at her like being modest was actually the right thing to do and he was proud that she was finally learning some manners. "You were the one who introduced us in the first place, after all! Now, come along. Both of you best get started before he gets too far or too lonely or too hungry."

Alice got up and the Mad Hatter pulled Tiger Lily's seat out from under her. Tiger Lily turned on him, knife in hand and ready to strike, when she remembered why she was doing this. She backed down. The Mad Hatter never let his smile falter.

"Come on, Witch of Wonderland," Tiger Lily said. "Try to keep up and we will make this quick."

Alice followed after her, though she wasn't entirely certain that Tiger Lily wasn't going to turn around and stab her in the night. Or while they were walking. That she wasn't going to do any stabbing at all, really. She seemed focused though, and put the knife away as she took to the woods, looking around for signs of the Jabberwocky. Alice stayed back and let her work.

"You could run," Tiger Lily said. "You can escape when you wish."

"I could," Alice said. "But I'm worried. The Jabberwocky can't be left to wander around Wonderland on his own."

"You think a dragon is a pet as well?" she asked, the accusing tone back in her voice.

"That dragon's already caused a lot of problems in Wonderland," Alice told her. "Do you already know what happened to the March Hare and the White King? Why they're like that?"

"They live, but it's like they have had their insides removed."

"Their hearts are gone. That's what happens here if you take out someone's heart. Before, the Queen of Hearts was using the Jabberwocky to take out the hearts of everyone in Wonderland one by one. She's learned how to do it on her own since, but I think the Jabberwocky might still be able to do it. I don't want him wandering around with no food and suddenly get the craving for hearts again."

"It is responsible for them?" Tiger Lily asked. "And that mad man still wants it to return? And you would trust it in his hands?"

Alice smiled. "Good, you're learning to ask questions. The Jabberwocky doesn't like Wonderland much, I don't think. But he stayed with the Mad Hatter for a while. Willingly. I don't know why, but if he doesn't like him anymore, I'm not sure where he'll go. Someone needs to make sure he's eating something other than hearts."

"It doesn't sound like a creature that is native to this land," Tiger Lily said. "It seems strange that such a creature would exist when there are so many talking animals. Does this Jabberwocky speak in riddles as well, or will we be spared?"

"He just growls and makes dragon noises," Alice said. "Are you finding anything?"

"We will not lure out the creature if you continue to speak so loudly," she said.

"Oh, I know how to call him back already," Alice said. The words were still in the back of her mind when she said it, but Tiger Lily snapped up and stared at her, falling silent in the quiet woods. Alice took a seat on a large rock. "I wanted to ask you about something else, though, before you go bringing the dragon back."

"You know how to call a dragon to your side?" she asked. "And you still claim not to be a witch?"

"You said you didn't trust me because I didn't ask you to do anything after last time, right?" Alice asked, ignoring her last statement. "I've been trying to find these two boys. They're twins. Both of them look alike. Well, technically triplets, but I already found one of them."

"And the witch is after three young men for herself," Tiger Lily said with a clear tease in her voice, her grin widening. Alice thought comments like that would get you turned into a toad from a real witch, but Tiger Lily wasn't concerned. "So greedy."

"They fell into Wonderland months ago. Dark hair, about

this tall, dress strangely for this world. They can speak in riddles too, but they won't be the same kind as the ones here. They might try to convince you to make a deal or trick you into something, but they actually do it intentionally."

"And if I find them for you?"

"Debt repaid?" Alice asked. "I did help you find food. And I'm about to help you find a dragon and take all the credit for it. Although…"

"You do not know if you want to find this dragon."

Alice let out a breath. "I just can't figure out why he ran off in the first place," she said. "I thought he liked the Mad Hatter, but if he's going to keep running off, then I don't know if it's really worth bringing him back to the Hatter at all. There has to be a reason he ran away and a reason he doesn't like the Hatter anymore. *Besides* the obvious," she added at the end, seeing Tiger Lily about to say something.

"It does not sound like a creature from this place," Tiger Lily said again. "It acts too much like an actual creature and not with enough madness. Are you certain it came from this land?"

"It has to be," Alice said. "See, it came out of this book."

Tiger Lily stopped at that, looking straight at Alice at her full height.

"It's my fault," Alice continued. "Cat made me read the first page and it let a whole bunch of stuff out of there. After. I mean, I only have the book because I stole it from the Queen of Hearts because she was going around and stealing the hearts out of everyone in Wonderland, and then the Cheshire Cat just kept chasing me around until I read that first bit of the book and it let out all this stuff. But the book was from Wonderland, right? So the Jabberwocky must have been from Wonderland too. I mean, I know he doesn't really make sense here. Or rather, he makes too much sense and nothing else around him makes sense. But he's from the book and the book is from Wonderland. Right?"

"You say there was a book?" Tiger Lily asked at Alice's imploring look. Alice nodded. "A book from Wonderland created a dragon?"

"Well, where else could it have been from?" Alice asked. "Who goes around making crazy books with dragons in them that drive people crazy?"

"Have you read this book?" Tiger Lily asked. She took a step away from her, but Alice didn't notice.

"Bits and pieces," Alice said. "I found something in it about calling the Jabberwocky, but some other stuff too. And other things that got released. I would bring them back to Wonderland too, but... It's complicated," she finished, not really sure how else to put it. "Very complicated."

"This book does not appear to have driven you mad," Tiger Lily said, relaxing as Alice curled her legs up to her chest on the rock. "Perhaps you should bring it with you when you return next. It will help to provide insight on the dragon. Perhaps there will be a way to put him back in the book if you look again. It will be a good reference should it get out of hand."

"Maybe," Alice said. "It couldn't hurt. And it works on Mark and Matt a little too if you change the words around a little, so maybe I could find them while we're at it. I just need to make sure no one else takes it while it's here."

"I shall assist you," Tiger Lily said. "Perhaps this book could even return the hearts to its people so there are far more frustrating people and animals that my people will be unable to hunt. While you are under my watch, the book will not leave you."

"Maybe," Alice said again. She checked her watch, finding she still had a little time before she had to be back, but she was already almost done. "You will keep an eye out for the guys, though, right? I have been looking for months, but I really can't find them anywhere."

"You have my eyes," Tiger Lily said. "I will soon be in debt to you twice. I always repay my debts."

Alice smiled, getting up off of her rock. "Then let's get a dragon!" she said, looking out into the forest. The range of the incantation was so much further in Wonderland and she was grateful for it. "*Ábedecian bealu gásric ælwiht hércyme,*" she called into the woods, looking to Tiger Lily. Alice reached behind her back and pulled out a coil of rope that she offered to Tiger Lily. "You might need this," she said.

Behind them, the Jabberwocky came crashing through the woods. Tiger Lily did not show any shock or surprise at the creature or his sideways snout as he came bounding forward, stopping shy of them by a good distance as he spotted Alice. She looked at him and met his horrible eyes, urging him to keep walking forward.

As expected, he hissed at Alice as soon as he got close. She stayed away and he kept his distance from her as well. He sniffed the air and his eyes landed on Tiger Lily, who did not flinch under his gaze. Alice could see that she had a hand ready to go for her knife, but she refrained and let him smell to his desire. Once he seemed content with her, he turned back to Alice, hissing and spreading his wings a bit to look bigger.

"This dragon does not appear to like you," Tiger Lily said.

"How very observant," Alice replied, trying to make sure Tiger Lily stayed between her and the Jabberwocky. "It doesn't seem to mind you, though. You should probably catch it now, before it realizes that you're going to tie it up."

It was an easy task. The Jabberwocky's hissing face never left Alice, though he didn't try to attack her. Alice kept him busy by moving slowly and staying out of his reach, but kept his eyes on her. Tiger Lily managed to throw a lasso around his neck and capture him in a leash.

"You need to teach me to do that one day," Alice said, smiling at how easily Tiger Lily seemed to get the hang of dragon wrangling. And that her knots were much better on the dragon than they had been on Alice.

While the Jabberwocky protested the rope, he protested everything else around him more and preferred the girl holding his leash that likely smelled like food with all her leather. Alice assumed she smelled like evil incarnate to him.

"I owe you twice, Alice of Wonderland," Tiger Lily said. "In return, I will do you two kindnesses. Be comforted that I always fill my debts."

"If you make sure the Jabberwocky doesn't run before I get back, that will be reward enough. If not, though, I might bring the book next time. Just in case. I know how to get it back if it's stolen this time, at least. Until next time, Tiger Lily."

Alice vanished, going back home where she managed to crawl into bed well before the sun rose for once.

CHAPTER 11

Library Time

THE LIBRARY WAS a comfortable place for Alice. She knew where everything was and she had a chance to think while she was putting away the books. Especially on a Saturday, when the only people in here were the people who had to be or the people who were panicked about something due on Monday. This was the easiest extracurricular activity Alice could have asked for. The librarians were nice and, after showing them the ropes, were more than willing to leave them alone to do the work.

Also, it was a great time to chat. So long as they were quiet about it, they could talk all they wanted.

"So do you know what part you got yet?" Alice asked Kevin as they went through a stack of books in the Biology section. She knew he'd only joined Library Club because he needed to do something if the play didn't work out. There was a chance he would drop this if he got a part, but she hoped he would decide to stay. She liked having the company.

"They post it today," Kevin said. "Heather said she'd check and come by to let me know. I hope it's just chorus or something easy."

"Imagine if you got the lead."

"I don't think they let you be the lead in the play right away," Kevin said. "And I messed up the audition pretty bad. I didn't quite hit the steps right and I was so flat. I should have practiced a little more if I wanted to get an actual part. There's really not much in Sweeney Todd for speaking roles."

"You were great, though."

Kevin smiled like Alice did when she thought someone was humouring her and went back to putting the books away.

Alice wanted to ask about that song he sung, but she kept quiet for now. She didn't really know much music outside of what Lori used to play and what her friends listened to, though Kevin rarely shared his collection of music. Since Kevin came from an international school in Korea, he might have different music that he wasn't comfortable sharing.

Alice could see the nervousness on Kevin's face about the play, though, so Alice stayed quiet and let him switch the subject as they kept working through the stack and the different sections. They talked about classes and how Robert was doing this semester, which was apparently much better. He'd fallen into whatever it was he did in his gaming club and actually found something that he was good at in his short time there.

They barely noticed the time until Heather came by the library and greeted them by smacking Kevin upside the head. It was the most at ease Alice had seen her lately, though she could still tell from the circles under her eyes that Heather's schedule was getting to her.

"Hey!" he snapped at her, then immediately brought his voice back down. "What was that for?"

"Getting it out of my system now," Heather said with a smug grin on her face. "At least until the next Combat Club when I can take it out on a punching bag with your face on it."

"What did I do?"

"Tobias," she said.

"What?"

"You got Tobias. You got one of the main freaking parts!"

Kevin stared at her for a long moment. "What?"

"Congratulations!" Alice chimed in. "Which one is Tobias?"

"He helps Mrs. Lovett around her shop and gets a solo," she added, glaring at Kevin, who still looked like he was in shock. "Pretty good for someone who had to be threatened into an audition."

"But I was flat," he said weakly. "And I messed up."

"Apparently no one else noticed," Heather said, still smiling. "You're too hard on yourself. You did great."

"What did you get?" he asked.

"Chorus," she said. She didn't sound sad about it. Instead, she sounded almost relieved. "That and victim number five. I think I get about two lines. Which I thought would be awful, but I have so much stuff for the other stuff I joined that it's kind of a relief that there's not too much to do."

"Does that mean you're going to die?" Alice asked.

"That is going to be fun," Heather told her with a broad smile. "But in the meantime, I am just going to have to try and be constructive with my jealousy of Kevin, here. Speaking of, Alice, are you making it to the next meeting?"

Alice shrugged. "I haven't checked my email yet."

"I hope so," Heather said. "It's fun, but it would be a lot better if I actually knew someone there. There's hardly any girls there and I kind of want someone who will spar with me."

Alice remembered the part of the club she was nervous about. She didn't really want to fight anyone. She just wanted to learn to not get hit. Still, she smiled. "I'll let you know as soon as I hear back from him."

"You better." Heather smiled and shook her head, looking up at the clock on the wall. "And I have to get to council.

Congrats, by the way," she said, smacking Kevin on the back as she left. "You deserve it!"

"I'm not sure that Combat Club is the best idea for her," Kevin muttered as he went back to putting the books away. "She hits hard enough already."

Alice shrugged. "It's fun," she said.

She could feel Kevin eyeing her as she continued to put the books away, but she tried not to pay attention. She let her hands keep moving and let her thoughts drift back to her hopes of Combat Club. On the permission slip, it said that it was a way for kids to learn self-defence, which was exactly what she was hoping for. She just wanted a way to stop getting thrown around or taken captive so easily.

And there was the chance to spend more time with Heather. Alice liked Heather and still felt guilty about leaving her roommate, Sarah, behind for the Bandersnatch. She wanted to make sure she was adjusting all right to having her gone. Heather might not even remember the other girl, but Alice was pretty sure Sarah would have kept her from taking on so much stuff.

"You know," Kevin said at last, "you could check."

"What?"

"Your email," he said. He pointed up at the clock on the wall. "We're done for the day. I can put these back and you can use one of the computers to check your email."

Alice stared at him for a moment. It hadn't occurred to her that the school computers could do that as well, but it made sense. "Thanks," she said, heading over to the computers and trying to remember how to get to her email as Kevin put the cart back.

It took Alice a minute to remember how to do everything, though she was already tempering her expectations. It had taken her father a week to even get back to her about his email, after all. He might not have had time since the previous night to read it. Just because it was the next afternoon didn't mean he had enough time.

As soon as she got in, though, there was a message from him waiting for her. She checked for an attachment first, ready to send that to the club, but there was no sign of one on the message. Curious, she opened the email.

I have already contacted the school to ensure you will not be participating in this excuse for an extracurricular activity. It's appalling they would offer it at all, much less that they would approach a young girl to join.

I expect better of you, Alice. Asking permission for something as violent and juvenile as this shows how little you have grown. Beating up classmates is for young boys who have yet to manage their anger, not a young woman. I hoped Lucena Academy was a better environment for you, but it is clear that you are not able to exercise the restraint I expect of you. You don't want to slip again, do you? You are aware of the consequences.

Alice didn't realize how high her hopes were to get into the club until they dropped. She looked at the email and kept her expression blank as she read the words. He didn't sign the form. She wouldn't learn how to defend herself or get away the next time someone grabbed her. She wouldn't get to spend any time with Heather to make sure she was all right.

And then there was Tasha. On top of being able to teach Alice to defend herself, it struck Alice that she might know Lori and might be able to tell her something about her sister's disappearance. She wanted another chance to talk to her, but without the club, Alice couldn't think of a reason to. She didn't even know she wanted to talk to her again until now.

"I'm sorry."

Alice snapped around and saw Kevin behind her. She quickly closed the browser before he could see anything about her slipping and ask what that was about. "It's fine," she said, keeping her voice steady despite her disappointment. "I've still got Library Club."

"It still sucks. My dad doesn't let me do a lot of stuff either, so I know what it's like. If you want, we could grab Robert and Adrianna and see if they want to do something. Get your mind off of it."

Getting her mind off of it sounded like a great idea. "I'll be fine," Alice repeated, getting up from the computer. "I think I'll just take a walk, though."

"Okay," Kevin said, moving out of her way as she got up and strode out of the library. He looked like he wanted to say something more, but Alice wasn't ready to hear it.

Alice knew just the place to go to make sure she wouldn't think about the disappointment at all. She would be too busy. Within a few steps, she was back in her room where a large purple cat waited for her.

"Alice," he said. "This place bores me so."

Alice didn't acknowledge him, reaching into the air and pulling the brown book out.

"Ah, but you are not bored at all, I see," he said, suddenly much more interested. He disappeared from the bed and reappeared around her shoulders "What has caused you enough distress that you might try to seek revenge of that sort? Or have you finally decided to try to save yourself?"

"Not today, Cat," Alice said, shrugging him off of her. She stepped through the mirror and into Wonderland.

CHAPTER 12

The Tiger Pounces

WONDERLAND WAS NOT big enough for her today. With the book in hand, she felt bold and reckless and determined to make the boys show themselves if she had to tear this whole place apart and tape it back together. She might even start trying a few new words out of the book to call them. She might as well. She'd tried looking everywhere else.

Alice needed to ask Tiger Lily for any news. Maybe she'd have some lead on them, but Alice doubted it. She was still too new to Wonderland and, while it looked like she knew what she was doing while she was tracking the Jabberwocky, it was hard to miss the trail it left behind. Maybe where she came from all of that looking at broken leaves stuff worked, but around here it was a very different sort of game to play if you were looking for anything.

It had probably also been less than a day.

Alice checked her wrist to find it bare. She forgot her watch today. She shook her head and kept moving. There was no rush for her to get back.

There was so much to do, too. Not only did she need to find the boys, but she should also check on the Jabberwocky. Since she needed to talk to Tiger Lily, she should probably check to make sure her tribe was doing all right. She said something about protecting the book as well and Alice knew she needed the help.

There was more than enough to keep her busy and her mind off of her disappointment.

She started at the Mad Hatter's tea party, though stayed only long enough to see that the table was abandoned. Alice didn't want to linger long enough for anyone to find her and rope her into a frustrating conversation, but she needed to know if the Mad Hatter still had control over the Jabberwocky.

A howl in the distance told her that no, he did not. She left the table before anyone could stumble on her and ran to the beast's cry. The Mad Hatter was there with the Jabberwocky on a leash, scolding him for being so unruly and telling him to behave himself.

At least he still had him. That was enough for now, she decided.

Alice went to White Rabbit's house next. "*Abedecian game-*

nian snytrian eormencynn hércyme," she called out and took a seat against the front door.

The house was empty but safe, and it gave her a spot to look up something that might be useful in trying to find Adrianna's brothers. She had all night, after all, and the day was beautiful as always. Even without Adrianna to teach her how to pronounce the strange words properly, she could stumble through them enough to make them work.

She was so used to the pages and their absolute nonsense to get through that she barely even needed the mirror anymore. She could read backwards at this point. She went through the random pages, wishing that there was something in here that actually was in the proper order. It was frustrating not knowing if the section she flipped to was going to be anywhere near correct.

She came across a page that had the words written in a spiral. She traced her finger along it to try and make out what was written and immediately put the book down on her lap, staring at the page.

Releasing the creatures in this book may cause the pages to warp and become difficult to read. If this should happen, pick up the book by the spine and gently shake out the pages. This will return them to their usual state.

It was so old that she feared the pages might fall out. She held it by the spine with the pages facing downward, not too high off the ground in case they spilled out, and gently shook the pages. The covers flew open and the pages inside spread out as she did so. She felt them tingle a little under her fingers and her hands numbed with each passing moment.

She watched as all her notes fell out and the words on the open pages spread until they turned the paper black. A moment later, the ink settled back into place as separate words and pictures on the pages. The pages fell back into place and the cover gently closed itself in Alice's outstretched hands.

She brought it back in and laid it on her lap, massaging the feeling back into her hands. "This book is so weird," Alice muttered to herself as she stared at the brown leather cover, waiting for another trick to come up. Maybe a new creature she could release if she said another nonsense poem that didn't fit with the rest of the book. Maybe something that would reach out and try to take her eyes if she stared too long.

She opened the book again and started flipping through the pages. They were all properly legible now, making for easy skimming to find whatever it was she wanted on the pages. Everything was in place and there was even a rough table of contents in the front to tell her where each section roughly started.

"You couldn't have told me this before?" Alice demanded of the book.

It said nothing back, but it didn't need to. The important thing was that she could actually make out everything in the book and figure out what to do with the Jabberwocky now. She might be able to even find something in here about how else to make Adrianna's brothers show up at her feet rather than running all over Wonderland looking for them. Unless they didn't want to be found.

They had to want to be found. Wonderland was no place for them. It was too dangerous for them to stay.

She stood up and looked around, listening for some sign of either of them. When there wasn't so much as a rustle in the underbrush, she moved on to the next spot and repeated the call. The candy lake had inhabitants, but they didn't have the chance to bother her before she took another two steps and appeared on the opposite bank.

She sat at the edge of the lake, not really sure how it fit in with the rest of Wonderland. Even for here it was a little strange. It was a pink lake that tasted like strawberry lemonade and the shores were something that she didn't want to taste. The whole thing was a bit like a candy factory exploded in a spray of colour. She wouldn't be surprised if this was where Wonderland's rainbows came from. If Wonderland had rainbows.

She read about the Jabberwocky while she waited to see if anyone would come to her. The page was still missing the picture of the Jabberwocky, but there was an outline there where the image once was, all the paper around it having yellowed while the lines still looked like new paper. In it, there was still a drawing of a knight, fighting and trying not to die, drawn in black.

According to the book, the Jabberwocky was a dangerous creature that was often placed in specific spots to ward away trespassers. There would be knights who would challenge it as a rite of passage, or to get to whatever it guarded, which usually involved treasures or damsels or things of great power. She wondered if it was just the Bandersnatch that waited on the other side every other time.

The claws had interesting magical properties to those who got their hands on them, as did much of the rest of their bodies. Their hides could make for excellent light weight armour and could be harvested as they shed rather than killing the creature to get them. The fangs were venomous and the book referred to a different section for a brief primer on what Jabberwocky poison did and how to counteract it.

Alice got up and looked around once she finished, feeling like she had learned a grand total of nothing useful. She never intended to let a Jabberwocky bite her, so knowing it was poisonous did her little good. And she already was fully aware of what the claws could do, having seen them in action first hand. It didn't say anything about how to get it to go back into the book.

She looked around for Mark and Matt around the shores of the lake, but she saw no one. Alice moved to somewhere with a table this time around to give it a shot.

She stood up and immediately took a seat at the empty table for the tea party. "*Ábedecian gamenian snytrian eormencynn hércyme*," she called again into the wild and went back to flip through the book. There was a whole section on vocabulary and a second one for spells and incantations that she could use, all centered around the beasts found in the first half of the book.

The problem, of course, was that they were sorted alphabetically rather than by usefulness. She skimmed through them to look for something she could use, letting her eyes drift and her mind catch on anything that felt important. She wasn't sure what she was looking for, exactly. Something to trap the Jabberwocky or something that would bring Mark and Matt out of hiding? Maybe something that would do both?

She had another thought. Going back through the bestiary of dangerous creatures or creatures with magical properties, she found the page for the Bandersnatch. The outline left at the top painted it as a silly looking creature, like a dopey lion instead of the monstrosity it really was. The entry was dense, but it didn't look like there was much actual information. The Bandersnatch was captured at great risk to everyone involved. It was unsafe for study, too powerful and too intelligent to be allowed to roam free. It made deals with people and tended to play with them like prey before taking something from them. It delighted in stealing loved ones and there was speculation that the Bandersnatch might have been an old god, brought down from the heavens and forced to hold a form.

"You shouldn't be reading that," a voice said from the table. Alice looked up to see the Dormouse snoozing in front of her. He spoke between snores, sounding like he was sleep talking, but Alice knew better. "We already have one mad woman trying to destroy things. We hardly need a second."

"I'm not really reading it," Alice said. "I'm just looking through it. There's a difference."

"There might be," The Dormouse agreed. "I suppose the words make for lovely pictures to look at."

"They do indeed," Alice said, closing the book and leaving it on the table in front of her. "I suppose you'd rather a conversation than watch me look through an old book."

"It would only be polite," he said. "After all, you have invited yourself to the table and proceeded to ignore everyone currently at it. This is really a new low for you, Alice."

That was more like the Wonderland she knew. "I've had a few other things on my mind. My friends are missing in Wonderland somewhere for one. The Jabberwocky started running away from the Mad Hatter. I don't suppose he's managed to figure out a way to make him stop doing that?"

"I suppose you wouldn't suppose that," the Dormouse said with a yawn. "Best not to suppose things that you have no business supposing. That is for the people involved to suppose about."

Of course. Alice looked over the table and found that no one was here but the Dormouse. "Where have the March Hare and the White King gone?" she asked instead.

"They went to retrieve their hearts," the Dormouse told her. "Terrible thing to have to exist without a heart. They were not whole, so they left to go and get the rest of them back."

Alice was a little sad to hear that. It wasn't easy to get the two of them out of the Queen of Heart's castle in the first place, but if she called them back, they would likely go back to the Queen. She had their hearts and the rest of them would follow her. Until someone could figure out how to put a heart back after it had been removed, she didn't know what else they were going to do. Alice was sure Wonderland could figure that out. After she found the boys and dealt with the Bandersnatch, she'd give them the book so that they could solve this.

On the bright side, at least the Jabberwocky wasn't really a priority anymore. While his claws were magical enough to remove hearts and his fangs were poisonous, his diet was limited to birds and anyone who attacked him. She hoped that the Mad Hatter taking him for a walk didn't constitute an attack.

"Oh good!" the Mad Hatter said as he came back from the woods, pulling along a very reluctant Jabberwocky on a rope.

Compared to his picture in the book, this Jabberwocky looked scared instead of awe inspiringly terrifying. He seemed more terrified of everything around him than before, his whole body balancing like he was ready to take off and his wings already starting to unfurl despite not having nearly enough space to take flight.

The Mad Hatter handed Alice the rope and the Jabberwocky hissed loudly at her. "Be a dear and make sure he doesn't run off again. I need to take a seat and have a cup of tea."

Alice looked from the rope in her hand and back up to the hissing Jabberwocky and back again. She took him over to a tree and tied the rope to that for now, leaving him off where he could hiss at her from a distance and she wouldn't have to worry about him randomly snapping her head off.

"Oh dear," the Mad Hatter said, looking at what Alice had left on the table. He picked it up and kept turning it over in his hands, running his fingers over the cover and never daring to open it. "My, is this what I believe I think it might be? Oh dear, dear me, Alice, do you know quite what this is?"

"She said she was only looking," the Dormouse chimed in.

"Oh hush you! I'm not talking to you!"

Alice snatched the book out from his hands and held it tight to her chest. "Yes, I know what this is," Alice said. "And I'm not going to be giving it to anyone else in Wonderland. We've already seen what it did to the Queen of Hearts, so who knows what will happen if I let one of you have it."

"I wouldn't dare dream of it, Alice," he said soothingly. "You know it drove her crazy. I had heard that she no longer had it, but I did wonder where it had gone. Last I remember, the Cheshire Cat had said something about going to find someone stupid enough to open it up and read it for him. He was so curious about what was in there to drive her so far. I never thought that you would have it. Who did the Cheshire Cat trick to get the book in your hands?"

"I got it from the Queen of Hearts," Alice said, shoulders falling. "The person he tricked was me."

"Well that's not very nice," the Mad Hatter said. "A young, sweet girl like yourself shouldn't be stealing things. The Queen of Hearts won't like a thief for a daughter very much and it wouldn't do for a thief to be a princess."

Alice's eyes narrowed on the Hatter. Why he thought she wanted to be a princess at all baffled her, especially the daughter of the Queen of Hearts. Besides, if she didn't take the book, she would have left Wonderland helpless at the hands of the Queen of Hearts. Without it, she seemed like she'd at least slowed down in collecting hearts, though Alice knew she hadn't stopped.

"I still have no intention to become the Queen of Heart's daughter," she said. "And besides that, Tiger Lily managed to be a princess just fine without being nice." She stood up and looked around, trying to find anything else moving around them. Nothing came up or down the path, nor was there any sign that the boys had found her at all. No reason to stick around any longer.

"If you'll excuse me," she said, walking behind a tree and coming out on the plains.

What struck her first was the breeze. It was welcoming and needed as she was starting to feel a little hot. She didn't know why, but she was getting angry again. She gripped the book tightly to her and wondered if this was going to be the start of her going crazy. She wondered if this was just because of her father insinuating that she was slipping again just because she asked to join a club.

Disappointment was nothing new, though. Her father had said no to her before, but there was something about this time that was bothering her. Maybe it was because she thought she'd been doing so well. Her parents didn't see much of it, especially since they spent so much time out of the house over the summer, but Ms. Miller must have told them.

She should have known better, though. Her father likely didn't want to see his daughter getting hurt in such rough conditions. There were so many boys in the club who were used to being much rougher than Alice was used to. She was likely to get very hurt if she did attend. Her father probably didn't think the risk of injury was worth the fun she might have. Not to mention she couldn't tell him why she really wanted to join.

Alice took a deep breath. When she got back, maybe she could ask Heather to show her what she learned. Alice only needed to learn a few things. She didn't need to attend the club for that.

"*Ábedecian gamenian snytrian eormencynn hércyme,*" she said into the field. She took a seat on the ground, hiding in the grass, and opened the book to the section on the Bandersnatch again.

The Bandersnatch was still her problem and she needed to know more about these deals or a way to trick him. Unfortunately, this idea that he might actually be an old god or a creature from the beginning of time looked like the only theory on him. There was nothing in here about how to get out of a deal.

The feeling of eyes on her made her look up from the book. From her place in the sea of yellow and green, she couldn't make out anything but the smell of grass. Nothing around her made a sound, and the grass didn't sway for anything but the wind. Still, she could feel something watching her and probably someone who was looking for her specifically as the feeling of eyes would not leave her.

"Hello?" she called out into the grasses, closing the book and getting to her feet to get a better look. "Mark? Matt? Is that you?"

There was no answer, but she didn't feel the eyes leave. It occurred to her that the eyes could be one of Tiger Lily's people on the hunt and she might have been mistaken for some of their prey. She started walking through the grass at full height so they could see her and made it obvious she was there. Someone was watching her and she wanted to be clear that she was not going to attack anyone and that she wasn't edible.

Alice emerged from the grasses by the creek where she'd found Tiger Lily the first time. The eyes were still there and watching her from what she could feel, but they had yet to make their move. She hoped they were friendly, but they weren't coming out of hiding yet, so Alice decided to take a break. It was calm here and she splashed a little of the water on her face and sat on the bank with the book on her lap.

It crossed her mind that the eyes could belong to Mark or Matt. Maybe one of them was watching her and checking to make sure their eyes weren't tricking them. After this long in Wonderland, they might be a bit more wary of random girls standing out in fields reading large, scary looking brown books.

Or they were considering whether to show themselves at all. She remembered Mike's hesitance to leave when she came for him. They might have found someone they were in debt to somewhere in Wonderland and were considering whether they really could leave before they repaid them.

Something passed by her ear and she let out a yelp of surprise. There was a small dart in the dirt across the creek now. She jumped back and another one joined it.

Whatever threw those, it was intentional.

"Tiger Lily?" she called hopefully. "Is that you? It's me, Alice."

Another dart came at her and Alice stumbled backwards, landing several feet away in the tall grass. Since when did anyone in Wonderland actually hunt her down and try to hurt her? Well, except that one time when she destroyed the White Rabbit's house by accident. She didn't remember any of that mob armed with darts being thrown at head height.

A part of her was hopeful that maybe it was Mark or Matt. That was who she had called and they had a very strange way of saying hello after spending so much time here.

Alice stayed very still on the ground, clutching the book to her chest and waiting to hear any sign of movement. It was quiet again, thankfully, and she didn't hear anything moving through the grass, or so she thought. The wind picked up and the rustling of the grasses grew louder than before, but nothing sounded out of place.

She never experienced Wonderland with wind before. It occurred to her that the wind was definitely new and only happened here in the plains. She wondered if the plains were actually a thing that always existed in Wonderland, or if they were some new addition as well, like those pirates in the Queen of Heart's dungeon.

She heard something crack in front of her and she bolted upright, her eyes peering out of the top of the grass and trying to find the source of the sound. "Ma—"

Her word did not finish and her hand slapped against her neck. Something pinched her. Between her fingers, she could feel the thin metal of a dart sticking out of her skin. A moment later, she was unconscious.

CHAPTER 13

Coming Undone

ALICE WASN'T SURE if she'd woken up at all. Her brain felt like it had turned into smoke that was slowly leaking out of her eyes and ears. She wasn't quite sure where the rest of her body was, but she was certain it was around here somewhere. It was probably just where she left it. Wherever that was. Maybe it had turned into smoke as well.

Her eyes drifted open and Alice had no idea where she was. It was the strangest room she'd ever been in. She was fairly certain it was a room, at least. The walls were white, but also brick sometimes. Sometimes they had terrible wallpaper on them. Sometimes they looked like bushes with flowers growing on them. Sometimes it looked like they were made of pink glass.

They kept moving as she looked at them. Sometimes they were close, other times so far away. The corners never stayed in the same place long and, from the corner of her eye, the ceiling kept flickering in and out of her vision. It was a room appropriately maddening for a place like Wonderland and she didn't like it much.

Alice gathered her arms under her head and pushed herself up. Despite how cloudy she felt, she was solid where the world around her was not. She could barely keep her head up as she watched the world continue to shift, but she forced herself to stay upright. She needed to figure out where she was.

She could pick out a few distinct places that the room kept turning into, many of them places in Wonderland that she had been before. There was the tea party, currently with several people gathered. There was a jail cell with the Jail Bird looking directly at her with suspicion on his face. There was the White Rabbit's house, empty though with a shadow moving through it.

The strongest version of the room was the white fabric tent that she didn't know. It was the one that kept coming back while the others shifted around her. It was a small tent with a table and chair and the brown book sitting on it. There was also a box that appeared to drip something, though Alice didn't know what.

In the white tent room, a young woman she could almost recognize sat on the other side of the table, watching. The room was filled with dense smoke that Alice felt herself becoming part of, all coming down from a basket hanging high above her. It was the only thing Alice could smell. The sweet scent of it, something that smelled like a forest she had never been to, filling her lungs was so pungent that Alice wondered if that was what was giving her such a headache. The eyes from the other girl stared at her, watching and waiting.

"Tiger Lily?" Alice asked. Her mouth felt like it was full of cotton and she wished she had a glass of water. She could almost see one on the table, but when she tried to stand, she fell back down. Beneath her was a small bed that she must have been sleeping on. She looked back to the girl on the other side. "Is that you, Tiger Lily? I don't... I don't feel well."

"You will continue to feel unwell for a long time," Tiger Lily said. "You are my prisoner."

Alice tried to get to her feet, but quickly fell onto her back. Her head spun and the room became every room all at once. She forgot which direction was up and she curled into a ball to wait for the spinning to subside. Slowly, she managed to push herself back up into a sitting position, now facing a different direction. She tried turning her head to find where Tiger Lily was, but a wave of nausea hit her and she nearly crumpled back down to the ground. Alice closed her eyes and waited for the world to stop spinning.

"My people are starving," Tiger Lily said, her voice coming closer. Alice couldn't tell if she was in front of or behind her. "I am sorry, but the needs of my people are stronger than any affection I might have for you."

"I can—"

"My people will not be fed by thieves," she said. "We have captured you and will use you as trade. You will learn how to return hearts to the people of this land and they will reward us with food that will not bring us harm. This has been decided by my father."

"Oh," Alice said. She had already forgotten everything that Tiger Lily said. Her head was swimming and her stomach was threatening to revolt. She risked cracking her eyes open and she could see the world changing around her. Below her, the shore of the candy pond appeared and Alice lost her balance. She landed back on the bed, but her hands were sticky and wet. She brought one of them up to her mouth, tasting the cotton candy water, but the tent remained.

"I am sorry," Tiger Lily said. She grabbed Alice under the arms and hauled her to her feet. The room spun and Alice couldn't stand, immediately falling forward. Tiger Lily caught her. Alice could feel her hands fade in and out of existence. She dropped Alice on the chair, the world around her still moving like a raging sea. Alice grabbed onto the table to try and steady herself, but she could feel it slipping through her fingers at times and solid at others. The room wouldn't stop changing around her.

Alice grabbed onto the edges of the table as tightly as she could and lay her head down, using the book as a pillow, and waited for it all to stop moving. It needed to stop moving. She couldn't do anything when it wouldn't stop moving.

It never stopped shifting and changing into other places. The throne room was there, as were the kitchens. She went through every room of the White Rabbit's house and the Duchess' fallen fortress. Everywhere she'd ever been, she was there again and gone a moment later.

And she was still always in that tent. It occurred to her that she wasn't going to be able to fall out of her chair and end up somewhere else. She was already everywhere else and she couldn't concentrate enough to take herself out of that tent anymore.

She could probably walk out of the tent. If she could just stand up without getting dizzy.

The world didn't stop moving, but Alice gradually found a way to exist within it, adjusting to sitting, and managed to push herself up. She stared down at the desk and waiting for it to come back into focus. It was a hundred tables all at once, but one of the versions was always there as everything else moved. The version with the book was always there with her and never moved away.

"You will find a way to return the hearts," Tiger Lily said. "You have two now. When you can return them to their bodies, we will send in more. When you are done, you will be released."

Alice didn't know if there was sadness in her voice or not. There was something there, but it echoed in her ears and she didn't know where it was coming from. Even though Tiger Lily was standing right next to her, it still sounded like she was so far away at times. And really close at others. Alice didn't know exactly where she was, but she looked like she was right beside the desk and nowhere at the same time.

Alice reached out and managed to grasp the glass of water that appeared in front of her. It became clear under her hands, like the table did when she laid on it. Not completely. It was still only half there, like holding a cloud, but she managed to bring it to her lips and drink a little before it dropped through her fingers and fell through her.

While she was aware that she should try to escape, Alice didn't even know where she was. The only thing that was clear was that incense burning high above her, emitting that smell that she couldn't place. It was strong and a little sweet, though very overpowering and entirely unpleasant. It seeped through her and she couldn't keep her thoughts in one place.

If she could come together enough, she would have felt fear. On some level, she knew that she was scared, but her brain couldn't hold everything together enough to understand all the pieces of her situation at once. She was trapped and couldn't leave.

On the desk, her hands were shaking. Alice knew she needed to pull herself together. She needed to focus if she was going to get out of here. She just needed to pay attention to Tiger Lily and do what she wanted.

Tiger Lily opened the book to the first page. "You will figure out how to put the hearts back. You say the Jabberwocky came from this book. You say that this book contains the secrets to the Jabberwocky. You will find the way to return hearts to the people so that my people may eat. We already barely sleep in the never ending sunlight. We need to eat. Read and learn and do. You will be set free when you are done."

Alice let her head sag to one side, trying to see if the words on the page would come into proper focus. She slammed her hand on it to stop it from slipping away from her over and over again. Slowly, the words started to come back into focus. She read them a few of them at a time, forgetting her place, and then going back. She used her finger to mark her place, but it kept falling through the page.

Free when she was done. She could go when she figured this out. She understood that much.

Alice's eyes drifted over to the box next to her and she felt her lunch start to come up right away. In the box, sitting side by side, were two still beating hearts. She lurched away from them, making the room spin around her. She was in a thousand different places, but she was always here next to the hearts. She tried to throw them away but her hand passed through them. She felt them pulse around her hand for a sickening moment before she fell off her chair.

On the ground, she might have thrown up. She didn't know. She didn't know what was happening. The hearts in the room made her think she was everywhere. She could hear them all around her for a moment, and then nowhere again. She kept moving no matter how still she tried to stay and nothing would stay in one place. She needed to get out, but she couldn't get herself together enough to go anywhere.

She was everywhere. Everywhere was right here.

Tiger Lily closed the box. "The hearts will remain here until you are ready to use them," Tiger Lily said. This time, she sounded quiet, but Alice could feel Tiger Lily pick her up and put her back on the chair. "When you can put them back and you are done, you will go free."

Put the hearts back and go free. The thought pulsed through her mind like a heartbeat. She stared down at the book and tried to make out the words.

CHAPTER 14

Missing Person

IT HAD BEEN almost a month since Alice disappeared, taking nothing with her. No one had thought anything of it until she didn't appear for class on Monday. She had a habit of wandering off on her own on the weekends without telling anyone where she went, but it had been too long to ignore her disappearance now. Everyone had been interviewed for some clue as to where she might have gone, but there were no leads.

There were stories, of course, to explain where she'd gone. The ghost from last semester had gotten her and now she was one of the ghostly figures that sometimes roamed the woods late at night. Cat, who had stopped showing up in his tree now that the weather was colder, had taken her away after she rejected him last year. Some people even wondered if she had been mysteriously pulled out along with her sister to go to school abroad in the middle of the semester. Others still thought they went the way of the two missing Case boys.

Alice's parents had yet to appear at the school to say anything, though word was that their lawyers had been deployed.

At this point, Adrianna was just happy that they stopped kicking her out of their room to go through Alice's side of it in search of some clue to tell them where she had gone. With Lance's help, she hid away all of Alice's diaries, knowing that Alice would not want anyone going through those. Adrianna found out on her own that the brown book was gone and that she'd forgotten her watch on the last trip to Wonderland.

School still continued, as did everything else, even with her missing. The excitement had petered off now that a few weeks had passed with no information and Adrianna was glad for it. She didn't know what to say to all these people who wanted to know what happened. She didn't know what happened in the first place. She was just lucky to have Heather and Robert keeping most of the attention off of her when they could, then Joe at choir practice when they would ask her there what happened.

Kevin was strangely quiet about it, though. He apologized to her once, though he wouldn't tell her why. She didn't think he knew where she was, but he was the last person to see her before she went missing. If he was anything like Adrianna, he probably thought he should have done something to stop her.

They slowly started to get used to their lives with Alice missing, all of them refusing to talk about Alice for a little while until they could figure out what to say about it. Instead, they kept conversation light, talking about how stressed out they were over finals or how the play rehearsals were going. Anything but Alice's disappearance.

"I don't get any of this!" Robert said, elbows slamming down on the table and fingers in his hair, his head leaning down over his history homework. "How am I supposed to remember all of this?"

"It's just dates," Heather told him. "It's not that bad. What's the part you're having trouble with?"

"All of it. I'm totally going to fail this."

Heather let out a deep sigh and went over to lean over his shoulder, going through everything with him very slowly. Kevin smiled sympathetically, but was too busy trying to help Adrianna work through her math homework to be of much help.

Adrianna felt the hand on her head and looked back to find one of her brothers standing over her. "Need to borrow my sister for a bit," Lance said to Kevin.

"Why?" Adrianna asked, packing up her homework. She threw it into her bag and waved farewell to her friends before turning back to her brother and falling in step beside him as they went to the stairs. "You haven't even said anything to me since you helped me put all that stuff away."

"I have a few questions about that," he said. Adrianna took the lead and went to her room to drop off her books. Lance took a seat on her bed, looking distinctly uncomfortable on it as he looked at where Alice used to live. Sometimes Adrianna wondered how long it would be before she could just call him Lance at school. This whole Mike and Mark stuff seemed kind of silly, especially now that there was only one of them left here.

"She's stuck in Wonderland, isn't she?" he asked, getting up to close the door. He was her brother, so they'd probably get nothing more than a small reprimand if they were caught. "That's where she went?"

"Well…"

"You can tell me, Addie," he said. "I've *been* there. I know what it's like. I won't go telling everyone about it. And I'm sure Alice wouldn't want you to be stressing out about this all on your own."

Her shoulders fell. She hadn't told anyone yet, but Lance did already know about Wonderland. And he was probably right about Alice not wanting her to worry about it all on her own.

"Yeah," she said quietly, starting to pace around the room. "She went missing on a Saturday. It's where she always goes on Saturday night. And she took the book with her, so she can't be anywhere else."

"Addie, it's been a month. Can't you do anything?"

Addie knocked against the mirror in frustration. "I can't do it like she can, Lance! It's just a mirror for me. And even if I could, how am I going to find her? She was looking for you for two weeks before she found you. She's still trying to find Adam and Matt. She knows where she's looking and it's still been months."

"Why's she even still looking for them anyway? They'll probably just show up on their own."

"She said it was her fault you guys fell into Wonderland so she's going to get you guys out."

Lance rolled his eyes. "They're going to turn up eventually. She's worried over nothing." He paused, his mind working out something that didn't seem quite right. No, they might not be all right. They were in Wonderland. But they were going to be fine. But Wonderland was dangerous.

"Are you okay?" Adrianna asked going closer to him, leaning in to get a better look at the confusion that spread over his face.

"Why didn't you talk her out of going back?" he snapped at her. His head was spinning, unsure whether to be worried or not, and he couldn't figure out why.

"Me?" Adrianna asked. "Why would I tell her not to go?

She doesn't even like going there! She's told me about all the awful things she has to deal with every time she goes back and how mean everyone is to her over there. It looks cool whenever I see it, but she keeps talking about how dangerous it is. And how would I stop her from going, anyway? She walks through mirrors to get there!"

"Fine, point taken," he said, leaning back on the bed and his mind working. "Has she ever been gone this long before, though? I mean, I don't remember her ever being missing long enough to call the cops before."

There was a knock on the door and Lance scrambled into the washroom to hide. Adrianna went to answer it, finding not an advisor standing there, but Evan. He looked unimpressed, arms crossed and looking out around the room. "Where is he?" he asked.

"What?"

"Lance," Evan said quickly. He didn't look at Adrianna, walking into the room and checking under both of the beds. "Where is he?"

"I'm thinking about going by Lance next semester, actually," Lance said, slipping out of the bathroom. "If I don't have Adam and Matt around, there's really no point in keeping up with the four letter M name thing we had going."

"You know the rules about the—"

"About the door," Lance said. "Look, I just wanted a private chat with my darling sister. I don't know if you've heard, but her best friend in the whole world seems to have up and vanished into thin air. I thought I should offer my condolences."

"That's not why you came in here," Adrianna said. She was rewarded with a sharp look from Lance, and a knowing one from Evan.

"I'm pretty sure I know why he was in here," Evan said. "Apparently someone's been snooping through the school files. They don't know who, but whoever did it was looking for a student that doesn't appear to exist in the database. The search term 'Cat' was caught a couple times. I don't know if you know anyone who that might pertain to, do you?" Evan eyed Lance, waiting.

"Oh hey," Adrianna said. "He might know how to—"

"Shut up, Addie."

"He might know how to what?" Evan asked, looking at Adrianna. "Addie, what is going on?"

"Don't pressure her like that, Ev," Lance said, trying to physically ease his brother away from Adrianna. "She's already been through so much and—"

"I can't cover for you forever, Lance," Evan snapped. "I'm graduating this year and you're going to have to actually stop getting in trouble every other week if you want to—"

"Hey, I haven't gotten in *any* trouble this year! Matt and

Adam are the ones who always want to go pull stuff. I spent most of the semester sitting in my room doing nothing."

"And I suppose you *still* don't know where they are?"

"They'll—"

"They are not turning up!" Evan snapped. "What is wrong with everyone? You and Adam and Matt just disappeared out of nowhere and everyone was concerned right up until we got home. Dad didn't even want to file a police report. It was like, that's fine, you're all okay, you'll just turn up. And *you*," he said, turning on Lance, "you were worried right up until we got home. You wouldn't tell me what happened, but you were practically panicking about where they were. As soon as we get home, you're just like everyone else."

Evan closed the door and turned to the two of them. "The wind closed it. No one noticed."

Lance grinned at that, but Evan rounded on him. "You are going to tell me what happened to you."

"I... what?" he stuttered, staring at Evan. "I was — I just — it was —"

Evan turned to Adrianna. "Adrianna," he snapped at her.

"Wonderland," Adrianna squeaked, scared in that moment of her brother as he stared her down. "He was in Wonderland."

"Adrianna!"

"He was being scary!"

"Would you listen to that? You scared her."

"What is Wonderland?" he asked, turning back on Lance. "You and Alice mentioned it before. Is that where Adam and Matt are?"

"I… it's going to sound completely insane, Ev."

"I've seen some things myself," Evan said. "And I'm getting sick of bailing you out when things go bad. The least you can give me is an explanation."

Lance softened at this, then that mischievous grin crossed his face. "Fine, but then you have to tell me what happened to you," he said. "I remember back when I first got out, you were asking her about whether I was somewhere and I still don't know why we have all those files about you on the drive."

"But we shouldn't be talking about Wonderland," Adrianna said. "Alice says only bad things happen when you tell someone about Wonderland."

"Don't you want to know what happened to Evan, though?"

"I already know that, though," Adrianna said.

Both of them turned to look at her. Evan was a bit more shocked than Lance at the revelation. "What do you mean you already know? *I* don't even really know what happened to me."

"Alice told me," she said. "And I helped her a little bit. Not much. She said she'd let me help that time, but then she went off on her own again." She squirmed under both of their accusing glares, wondering if she should have mentioned it at all. Alice never said anything about not talking about the Bandersnatch, though, just that talking about Wonderland gets you in trouble because no one believed you.

"Addie," Evan said slowly. "Do you know where Alice is?"

Addie hesitated, looking to Lance. Lance already knew about Wonderland, but she didn't know if she should keep telling more people about it. Bad things were not something she wanted. It was already bad enough having to talk to all those people who kept asking if Alice was on drugs or if she had a secret boyfriend that she didn't tell anyone about. She couldn't imagine how much worse they were going to get if she kept telling more people.

"Alice is in Wonderland," Lance said for her. "She's been going back a lot to try and find Adam and Matt. She apparently thinks they aren't going to come back, so she went looking for them again. And she hasn't been back since she went in the last time."

"And what is Wonderland?"

"I... don't really know," Lance said. "It's this kind of crazy place where there's a lot of people who keep telling you that you're rude over and over. And there's this evil queen that somehow removes people's hearts and keeps them so that they'll do whatever she tells them to."

"And you're saying Matt and Adam are there?" Evan asked. "And you aren't even a little worried about it?"

Lance hesitated. A mask of confusion fell over him as he tried to come up with an answer to that. On the one hand, he knew they would turn up eventually and that there was nothing to worry about. On the other, he knew Wonderland was incredibly dangerous and there was a very good chance that Adam and Matt could be in serious trouble over on that side. Lance was lucky to get out of there in one piece when he did.

Evan took the moment to turn to Adrianna. "Where is Wonderland? Can you get to it from somewhere on campus?"

"Alice could," Adrianna said, glancing at the mirror and avoiding his eyes. "She could make the mirrors show Wonderland and walk through them into it. But I can't do anything like that. I just watched her do it."

"And is there anyone else who can do that?" Evan asked.

"Funny you should ask that," Lance said, perking up. "See, funny story. When I first got thrown head first into that place, which makes our dear sister so nervous every time we mention it, it was right after we saw our old buddy, Cat. I was just looking him up to see if I could track him down, but it looks like he actually doesn't go to school here."

"You're not off the hook for going through school files," Evan said. "What does he have to do with Wonderland, though? I thought it was just a crazy place that wasn't here."

"You're taking this all really well, Ev."

"I've seen some stuff myself," he said, looking a little grim about it. "I'm still not quite sure what was happening, either. I've been meaning to ask Alice."

Lance leaned past him to look at Adrianna.

"He was taken by the Bandersnatch last year," Adrianna said. She frowned at him, but the Bandersnatch wasn't Wonderland, so it would be all right. "It made everyone forget that Evan was ever a person and he kept him in a garden of other people who were all turned into silver statues. Alice had to do a deal with him so that he'd let Evan go, so she moved all the Jubjub birds to keep people from getting close so there'd only be worthy people. She said there's still someone named Sarah there that she has to get out, though, but she took a break from trying to get her out to try and get Adam and Matt back."

"And she still took finals," Lance said, sounding a little impressed. "I would have just not bothered all together if I had to do all that. Wait, when were you missing?"

"So this Cat guy can go to Wonderland and find Alice?" Evan asked, ignoring Lance.

"They don't really get along," Adrianna said. "He kind of threatened her a few times, then trapped her in Wonderland once, then sent everyone into Wonderland because apparently she wasn't letting him leave in the first place. But I think he could probably find her if he wanted to."

"How do we find him?" Evan asked, looking between Lance and Adrianna.

"I found nothing," Lance said. "If it were warmer, I'd say check that tree, but I never found anything about a home address or anything at all on the guy."

"I don't think he minds me," Adrianna said. "Maybe there's a way I can call him and get him to come out."

Laughter echoed through the room that came from none of the Case siblings. "Ah, the pretty friend dares to think she is as interesting as dear Alice," he said, laying out on Alice's bed. His head and shoulders drooped off the side, looking at them upside down with wide purple eyes. "I've been so bored without Alice to tease that I am forced to take amusement in that. I should not feel so bad for my amusement, but it's been so lacklustre since she left. I must find a new toy or I fear I may die of boredom in this place."

Adrianna started to get up, but Lance pounced on him. Cat slithered away as Lance grabbed his ankle. He ended up with only a shoe in his hand, the rest of him having vanished. He stared at the shoe in his hand for a long moment when he heard Evan make a noise behind him.

Lance looked behind him and his vision was filled with Cat's face staring directly at him, his grin too wide and looking at him as a cat might regard a mouse. "Oh my, has something finally come along to entertain me?" he asked no one at all.

Lance backed away with the shoe and Evan jumped in, grabbing Cat and pinning his arms behind him. Cat looked bored at the attempt and slipped out, appearing behind Adrianna and looking her over. Both of the boys stopped their attempts to assault Cat for the moment as Adrianna turned to face him.

"This one would never harm me, though," Cat said, grinning wide as he looked her over. "Their game is so easily foiled by how timid the youngest one— *urk*!"

Adrianna grabbed him by the tie and pulled him down to face her. Behind her, both of her brothers stared in shock at her. They had never seen her lift so much raise her voice before, not even in her own defense. Now, she looked Cat in the eyes and made him maintain the contact, not shying away or backing down from him.

"We're looking for Alice," she said, her voice not any darker or angrier than usual. "You can at least show us where she is. She said you were better at this than she was, after all."

"Oh did she now?" he asked, speaking directly to Adrianna for the first time instead of as an object in the room. "I suppose I may be so inclined, if there were some adequate reason for me to lend my gracious and vast services. It is never good for one to provide a service free unless they intend to provide that service free for all eternity, after all."

Adrianna didn't remove her hand from the tie, but his

head faded out of it and his neck leaned back before his head reassembled on his shoulders. She was left with a loose tie in her hand that was no longer around a neck, but Cat smiled as he looked back at her. He was willing to negotiate now.

"But what could you possibly have to offer me?" he asked. "There are not a great many things that I could possibly want. I already have most things I could ever need. I am a cat, after all. My needs are simple and my pleasures eloquent and elegant. You would need to provide me with something quite delightful in order to make me oblige you in even this most simple of tasks."

Adrianna looked at him, going through everything she had and trying to think of something that he could possibly want. There wasn't that much she had with her. She didn't bring much with her to school and even the things she left at home were probably nothing that a cat could possibly want. She might have a ball of yarn somewhere, but she couldn't imagine he'd want that as he was now.

"Forget him, Addie," Lance said, dropping down onto Alice's bed with the Cat's shoe in his hands. "He probably can't do anything."

Cat twitched, his eyes finding Lance. Those eyes slid off of him a moment later and went back to Adrianna. "Interesting pet you have there," he said.

"I haven't ever seen him do anything worthwhile," Lance

said. "I mean, yeah, sure he *says* he threw me into Wonderland, but can we really be sure about that? Alice was there too. It might have just been her doing that by accident. And I know she accidentally does that. He's probably just taking credit for an accident."

"It is quite a loud toy," Cat said, his smile and grin getting even wider. "Perhaps you best shut it up. I would much rather be hearing from you and what you would offer me for my services."

"Services that he can't prove he can provide," Lance said in a sing song voice. "He talks big, but he's useless. He teleports good, I give him that. Better than Alice. But looking into Wonderland? Opening up a way there? I'd like to see it."

In an instant, Lance and Cat were gone and there was a clatter at the dresser. Cat held Lance by the neck, Lance desperately trying to keep hold of Cat's arms to keep from falling or choking in his grip. Lance's head dipped through the mirror and into Wonderland.

Adrianna recognized the courtyard of the castle. The greenery was more charred than she remembered it, like something had set it on fire and they were still trying to rebuild it, but it still looked just as magical as she remembered it.

"Your toy is about to win himself another visit to Wonderland for his rudeness."

"Don't!" Adrianna pleaded. "He didn't mean it. I'm sure

you're a very good cat that can show us Wonderland just fine without any problems at all."

Lance risked a look into Wonderland and choked out, "You didn't even show Alice."

Cat let go and Evan ran forward, grabbing Lance as he fell backwards through the mirror and pulled him back into the room. Cat glared back at the two of them, then at Adrianna who was now looking at the mirror.

"He's right," she said. "Alice isn't there."

Cat stared at the mirror, twitching and looking carefully. "She moved," he said, half as an excuse, half curious to himself about the matter. "Now where did she go?"

The scene moved to a table in the ruins of a large stone building and there was a faint impression of Alice for just a moment before it faded away. It came back a moment later a little stronger, and then it was gone again.

Cat moved the image in the mirror. This time, it showed a table with the Mad Hatter looking overjoyed, having a delightful reunion with a very large hare that was his own size. Alice flickered into the scene again, completely translucent and tried to reach for one of the crumpets on the table. She picked it up and managed to bring it a little closer before it dropped out of her hands and she was gone.

"Strange, strange," Cat said. Lance opened his mouth to say something, but Evan covered it to keep him quiet. "What is that girl doing, spreading herself across Wonderland like that? That is not how treacle is meant to be eaten. You do not share it, you keep it for yourself."

Finally, after several more scenes where Alice was only a faint image that flickered away after a moment, he managed to find one where she was still there. She was still solid as smoke, parts of her becoming more faded at times than others and looking to be in a constant state of flux.

She was collapsed over a table, reaching out for something that she couldn't quite get. She managed to get a hold of the crumpet, bringing it close and taking one bite before her shaking hands dropped it and it vanished. She kept trying to push herself up to sit, but she wouldn't stop shaking. Sometimes her hand passed through the table completely and she slammed back down onto the surface, but she kept trying.

Next to her was a small box of something that looked an awful lot like hearts. They pulsed in a rhythm next to her, not bleeding through the box or moving at all except for the cons-tant beating.

"If you want a reward then save her," Adrianna said. Alice didn't look like she was doing well at all, but Adrianna didn't know what to do to help. It wasn't just the fact that she looked like a ghost, but the circles under her eyes and how much she shook.

Lance kicked out as Cat leaned closer to the mirror to

study the scene. Cat didn't try to stop himself from falling forward into the mirror. As he passed through, he changed from being the strange Lucena Academy student with the inappropriate colouring to a large, fluffy, purple cat with spiral stripes.

They stared as the mirror faded back into a regular mirror. Lance realized it was a bad idea as soon as he had done it, but he had to do something. They stared in silence for a long moment before Evan finally spoke.

"Did he just turn into a cat?"

CHAPTER 15

A King's Rescue

ALICE DIDN'T KNOW how long she spent there in that tent with the incense burning above her, keeping her in a fog that she felt part of. She barely even knew where she was anymore, not having left the desk except to fall onto the bed behind her. No food was ever brought, but sometimes something appeared in front of her that she could eat if she could keep it still long enough and it didn't try to escape her.

There was nowhere but this room to her anymore. She couldn't remember anything outside of here. There was no world that was outside of this place. This place was already so many places, constantly becoming other places, but also always just a tent with the incense burning high above her. She didn't even know if the other places she saw were real, or if the tent with the incense clouding her mind was.

Sometimes she was worried about other things, but she

couldn't remember what those other things were. All she had to do was figure out how to put the hearts back into people. When she finished that, she would be free to go. The answer was in the book in front of her, and so she had read all of it. There was so much information in it that she had trouble getting through it all. The words kept swimming off the page and the world would start spinning if she moved too much. It rocked when she turned the page.

She was used to the constant shaking now. She couldn't remember a time when she didn't shake anymore. She didn't know how long it took, but there was always at least a slight trembling. If she was lucky, that would be all it was. Everything shook as it shifted and moved around her, but she had to get used to it. Eventually, it was all normal. She did not know how she would adjust if it ever stopped.

Her name left her a lot. She couldn't remember all of it anymore. Tiger Lily knew the first part of it and would remind her, but it hardly seemed important. All that was important was the book. When she figured out how to make the book tell her how to release the hearts, then she would be closer to leaving the room and seeing what was outside of here. Something was outside of here and Tiger Lily made it sound like it was something that she wanted, so Alice believed her.

She made progress, though Alice didn't know how long it took. There was another book that she needed to consult that would have an answer. She remembered slurring the words to Tiger Lily, not really remembering at that point how to talk. There were so many words in her head. Too many words and not enough that she remembered how to say. She had to point to the book where it said what she needed. She needed a chapter from a red book. After that, she had been left alone for a long time with nothing to do. She kept reading the brown book over and over again until Tiger Lily finally returned.

She learned a lot of things from that brown book. Her mind filled with that information. She started memorizing whole sections that she could repeat back to herself when she eventually collapsed or fell over, which she did sometimes. Sometimes she moved her head and the world spun and she could focus on the pages she memorized in order to wait out the dizzy times and the times when the table stopped being there for a minute.

Alice did not count the days. Days had no meaning to her. She could not count either, so the numbers meant nothing. She did not waste her time trying to remember the numbers. There were too many numbers and she knew a way to tell when a day had passed. Tiger Lily would come in once a day, and when she appeared it was a new day. This Alice knew. This was all Alice really knew.

Sometimes she was jealous of Tiger Lily. She was always so upright and able to walk. Alice couldn't remember what walking was like. She clawed her way up to the table to read the books when she fell over. There was a bed below her, but the rarely slept. She needed to keep reading the book. The book would make her go free. She would just need to finish what they wanted her to do and she would be set free.

She did not know what she would do when she was free, but it was a thing that she was supposed to want. Tiger Lily said she wanted to be free, so she wanted to be free. For all of this to end. That was all she needed to know. That was all there was for her.

Alice didn't know what it was to be free anymore. She didn't think much about the future or escape or the end. There was only the book.

When Tiger Lily returned, she did not return with a book. Tiger Lily gave her several sheets with writing on them instead. Alice was told this was just as good. She would need to use these pages from the book instead and so she started to read the new pages. They were about hearts and what they did and how they fit and putting them back once they were removed. She wasn't sure why she was looking this up most days, but she read them with the pages from the brown book about the special changes she would need to make to accommodate for the special way they were removed.

The box with the hearts always made her nervous. She learned that if she left the box alone to leak on the table, it would not so much as emit a heartbeat. Now, though, she needed to open it and look at the beating hearts. Her own jumped at the sight of them and hammered harder in her chest when the box was open, but she had to do it. It was the only way to be free.

Tiger Lily opened the box for her when Alice was ready. She started trying what the book told her to, but she couldn't bring herself to do more than move it barely an inch. She would try again and again until the fear got the better of her, but they would only lift a little before dropping back into the box.

She couldn't close the box again when she was done because her hand would pass through it. She tried to pick up one of the hearts and throw it away, but she could feel it pulsing around her hand as she passed through it. The fear of them made her dizzy and sometimes she fell over trying to make them go away. Sometimes she fell into the hearts. She learned to stop being scared of them.

The box was never closed again once it was open, serving as a constant reminder to Alice of what she had to do. Some days she still needed Tiger Lily to remind her what she was doing. She needed to put the hearts back in the people. These hearts were to go back in their proper places. The papers and books in front of her told her how to do it, though she could not make it work yet.

The instructions on the paper made her tired and she slept sometimes. When she did, she would wake up in her bed and have to crawl back up into the chair and try to remember why the hearts were there all over again. That book was all there was in her world. She wanted only to read it. If she read it she would be allowed to go. If she figured out their puzzle, she would be allowed to go. She didn't know what else there was to do. Her entire purpose in life was to just figure out how to put the hearts back.

She thought some days she had it. There were instructions here on the desk with the hearts. She knew what she was supposed to do and she wanted the hearts to leave forever. She didn't know why, but she was convinced the hearts were here as a way to make sure she behaved and kept doing exactly what she was supposed to do. They were watching her and would attack her if she dared to not do what she was supposed to do. She knew they would. If she tried, she could even remember them doing it.

Alice managed to memorize the thing she was supposed to do. There were things she had to do with her hands and things that she had to think about and things that she had to say in words that she didn't recognize. She didn't know how she was going to do it all. She could barely move without falling over and it was hard to think of other things or even speak. She started muttering things, her words quiet and strained at first until she finally managed to make them come out properly. She did this while staring down at the pages, remaining perfectly still. Her voice was hoarse and every word tore at her throat like knives.

Water appeared before her one day. It took her a few tries before she got a small drink from it. And then she tried again with another glass for one more small sip. And another. She fell over between each of them from the effort, but she ended up with just enough so that she could actually make her mutterings turn into her voice. The water fell through the pages whenever she dropped it, but she didn't mind.

It had been so long since she heard her own voice that she wasn't sure who was speaking at first. It didn't matter. She tried the words. They were strange and foreign, but parts of them were familiar. She knew which sounds were wrong. There was another voice in her head there, correcting her. It was nice and friendly and strangely familiar. She didn't know who it was because it didn't sound like Tiger Lily, but the voice helped her figure out how to say the words.

The hands were harder. Tiger Lily was there to watch her for some of it, picking her up when she fell and suggesting she stop for the day. Alice didn't stop, knowing that this was how she was supposed to get free.

She was getting so close. She knew that she needed to do this. She had to move her hands around. Small circle over the hearts. Big circle to send them out. Small over the hearts. Big to send them out. She kept trying until she stopped falling.

The last one was holding the image in her mind. She did this separately too. Part of her mind was spent making sure she stayed sitting and the other part was on being conscious. She didn't know which part she would dedicate to thinking of the people the hearts belonged to. Of asking which creatures they belonged to first, then sending them back out afterwards, then holding the image of the heart in its proper place after she was done. It was a lot of things to think.

When she tried the first time, she closed her eyes and tried to come up with each image. The first one came, but she opened her eyes to find herself on the ground. She had forgotten that she was supposed to be sitting. She would remember that the next time, she hoped.

She spent time holding those images in her mind, practicing and practicing until she could do it without falling off her chair until the end. Once she managed it, she tried with her arms. She didn't finish the first big circle before she was on the ground, her head spinning and mind devoid of what she was supposed to be thinking about.

Alice took it in pieces, putting each part of the instructions together one bit at a time. It was easier to start with the words and the thoughts together. With both of those, she could use her hands to keep her balance. Once she had that, she was ready to try the last of it.

When she was ready to try it, she turned in her seat to the hearts in the box. They were sitting there, beating as they always did. The beating always made her think of them all around her, looking at her. The room shifted so that there were so many hearts everywhere, all beating at her, all ready to jump on her and attack her for not concentrating right.

It took her a while to try and sit in front of them without thinking of the hearts trying to attack her. There were so many. They all wanted to kill her and she didn't know what else she was going to do about it. She needed to leave so that they would not chase after her. Or maybe they would let her leave if she got rid of these two and these they would stop calling their friends over.

Tiger Lily was there when she tried. After watching Alice fall over trying to move her hands and speak and think all at the same time, she moved behind her and held her under the arms to keep her up. Alice managed to stumble through the words the first few attempts and forcing the phrases out of her mouth until she could say them coherently. She concentrated hard until the thoughts formed right in her mind.

Finally, she felt it work. She felt something catch on her hands that followed into her brain. She saw two peo-ple, one for each hand. The March Hare was on one of them and the White King was on the other. She kept her mouth moving, her tongue going more smoothly now that it was working. The spell seemed to be helping her as she kept going. She moved her hands out in a wide circle, feeling Tiger Lily grab her again as she was about to topple over, and she felt the hearts fly off with the tips of her fingers.

She kept her hands out wide as each heart found their owner. She could feel them hunting until they finally landed on their proper person. Once they were there, Alice twitched her wrists and the hearts returned to their proper places.

There was commotion outside the room. Tiger Lily managed to lay Alice down on her bed before she ran out. Alice didn't know if the commotion was because of anything she had done or not. She was tired and she needed to sleep. She couldn't focus on anything. Tomorrow, she would go back to reading the book. The new things she did were far too exhausting.

She woke up and the next day didn't come for a while after that. Tiger Lily didn't appear, but she got up and went to the desk anyway. She looked at the box and the hearts were gone. She didn't know what to do without the hearts there, so she went back to reading the book and the pages again. The book would know what she was meant to do. She could count on the book to be there. At least until Tiger Lily came to tell her it was a new day and what she should do with it. She had forgotten why she was there.

She flipped through the pages as best she could. The movements still made her dizzy, so she moved slowly. There were no hearts left on her desk, though, so she did not know if she was supposed to do this. Something was supposed to happen when the hearts were gone. Free? Was she supposed to be free now? Tiger Lily would tell her when she came.

The day was very long because Tiger Lily did not come for a very long time. When she did appear, Alice mumbled something in question and gestured at the box, earning herself another wave of nausea. The words mingled around in her head, sounding like nonsense until she could sort them out. It took her a few tries until she managed to ask her, "What do I do?"

Tiger Lily came by her desk and knelt down so that she could look Alice in the eyes. "Now, Alice of Wonderland, you will need to continue to put hearts back," Tiger Lily said very slowly. "When you have finished doing that for all of the hearts, then you will be free."

Alice did not nod, only staring at her in dull recognition, trying to parse the words out. She finally managed to get them all sorted out while still staring at the same spot well after Tiger Lily had left. She was getting dizzy again so she put her head down, only to fall completely through the table and bash her head against the ground. She stayed down until she could remember which direction up was. Once she remembered, she crawled back up to the desk.

She went back to the book. The book would be what she had to do. There was only the book and nothing else. She would need to find the pages about the hearts again. When she found those pages, she could learn more. If she did more at once, she would be free sooner. She did not remember what free was like, but she wanted it. Tiger Lily said it was good.

Something fell in front of her. Blearily, she looked up and the room spun around her again. The movement was too much and she had to wait for her eyes to readjust before the thing in front of her slowly became a purple cat staring at her.

She knew this cat, but she didn't know why.

"I do believe you need to teach that pretty little friend of yours some manners," he said. "Her and that pet of hers. Oafs and buffoons you go to school with."

Alice stared at him. He was speaking too quickly and using words that she didn't quite remember. She didn't know what he wanted or what he was talking about, only that he was not happy. She did not know what she was supposed to do about him, so she continued staring at him.

He started to fade away as he paced across the desk, but stopped. "Isn't that curious?" he asked, looking about the room. He did not sound happy. "So is that it? They have captured you with nothing. This is why you've found no mirror to make your escape though you have appeared before several. This is how you have spread yourself so thin. By trickery."

The cat wobbled in front of her. It was hard to watch him trot back and forth across the ground, unable to quite find which way was forward and backwards, but she knew what that was like. There was no up or down. He started to get harder to see, his edges all getting fuzzy and out of focus. He stopped moving after a while, settling on a spot on the ground and staying there.

"A mirror he says," another voice said behind her. This one she definitely did not remember, but she did not turn around. She was already leaning over the table, she realized, head balanced on her arm and watching the cat sideways. She couldn't hope to sit properly right now.

Something grabbed her from behind and she tried to grab the book, finding it firm in her grasp. She pulled it close, still open to the page and crumpling it against herself as the hands pulled her out of the seat and dragged her backwards. She did not resist, the world around her moving violently. She lost focus on where she was and closed her eyes to block out everything around her. She felt the person's grip on her falter, her arms and body slipping through as he kept trying to drag her.

"Oh, focus girl," the man muttered to her. "I am trying to save you. I am in your debt and a king will always pay his debts."

Alice did her best. With her eyes closed, she could better focus on staying close to the hands and the arms around her. At the very least, she could focus on being in one place instead of all of them. It seemed to get easier and they passed under a curtain, through the trees, and smashed through a brick wall all at once to arrive outside where the sun was shining.

Sun. She knew sun. It was warm. She knew this feeling. She missed this feeling.

Then they went inside again, through another wall, under a waterfall, and undersea, to another room that was bigger than the last. It still kept shifting and changing, moving around and around until finally he brought her in front of a mirror.

There was a king holding her, Alice saw, and she looked like she wasn't quite there. Or he wasn't. There was a mirror in front of her that always looked like a mirror, but it was a different mirror each time. She didn't know what to make of any of it.

"How do you use this to go home?" the King asked her.

She stared at the mirror, her mind sticking on one word. Home. Home was a word she knew. That was a place she knew. Had she done what she was supposed to do? Was this what free was? Was she allowed to go home?

The mirror in front of her turned into another room. It

was solid in every mirror and she could see people in it. She knew those people. She focused on one of them. One of them was familiar. She had a name, but Alice couldn't remember it right now. She felt so dizzy from moving that she couldn't make herself understand what was happening. She shook too badly to get to her feet like the King was trying to make her do.

"Consider my debt repaid," the King said as he threw her into the mirror, picking up her feet and flipping her the rest of the way through.

She crashed over several things on her way down to the floor, where she eventually settled again. She clutched at the book in her hands. There was the book. She knew the book. The book was important. She could do things with the book like read it and do things people asked of her.

There were people around her. They crouched around her and said things that she couldn't make out because they were all talking on top of one another. She was dizzy and one of them tried to take away the book. She let them, trying to find something to focus on. The room would not stop spinning.

A thought occurred to her as she lay there, and then was moved up to her bed. The room wasn't changing as much here. It moved a little, but not like before. It was only a little. She could see a different forest sometimes, the cafeteria sometimes, but usually it was just the room.

She had done what they asked her to do. She finished the task. And now she could go, and someone had taken her so that she could go.

She was free.

CHAPTER 16

Road to Recovery

ALICE SPENT NEARLY a week barely conscious and trying to recover from starvation, severe dehydration, and exposure to something that they could not place in Lucena Academy's hospital wing. She'd proven impossible to move to a hospital, with every attempt on that first day ending in her partially conscious body appearing back in the hospital bed. They were fully equipped to deal with her, so she was allowed to stay there with a doctor and nurse consulting from the hospital, provided she didn't get any worse.

By the second week, she was doing much better. The hospital staff deemed her well enough to be left in the hands of the school nursing staff. She had a string of visitors, though it was still tough to keep them all straight. Adrianna was there, trying to see if Alice was getting any better, which she was. There were investigators that asked where she was and what happened, to which Alice replied that she couldn't remember. Her friends were there, and Adrianna's brothers had come by. Mike and Evan in particular looked relieved that she was doing well. Someone told her they had been the ones who found her.

Someone called her parents, who did not make an appearance. They didn't even call Alice, leaving a message with Miss Amanda telling her that she would not be returning to school next semester. Disappointed though she was, she couldn't say that she was surprised by it. She was gone for a month with no explanation.

"How are you feeling today?" Miss Amanda asked, bringing breakfast in for Alice.

"Better," Alice said with a smile. She came to really like Miss Amanda, who was quick to put a stop to any questioning that looked like it was causing Alice any distress. They tried to send her away, but she had the administration behind her. Given that they wanted to salvage their missing student case as best as they could in the eyes of the other parents and students, she was allowed to look out for Alice.

"After you finish, we'll wait an hour and see how you do on your feet," Miss Amanda said. "If you pass, today, you're free to head back to your dorm."

"Free," Alice muttered, laughing a little to herself and shaking her head. All she wanted for a month was to be free, but she didn't even remember what it was. Now that she was out, she'd been confined to the bed and interrogated. This was hardly the freedom she had asked for. Still, she ate as she needed to and was glad to not be dizzy and shaking constantly. And she probably could run out of here, but she was a little teleportation shy after the last month of phasing in and out across Wonderland.

When she was done, she got out of the bed on her own, Miss Amanda there and ready to catch her if she fell. She had fallen several times attempting to get out of bed already, but the past couple days had been better as she was getting steadily stronger. She walked on her own to the treadmill and started to walk.

"Looks like you should be ready to go today, Alice," Miss Amanda said, smiling. "A shame we won't be seeing you next year."

"I'm sorry," Alice said.

"Oh don't be," she assured her. "Your blood work and samples came back clean. No drugs, no alcohol, nothing suspicious except the smoke inhalation. There's a note saying cedar here, but I don't know why they thought that might be important. You still don't remember what happened?"

"No," Alice said, still a little wary about shaking her head. She wasn't all the way better yet, but she wanted to get out of this hospital wing. She needed to figure out some way that she could set the time back so that she could stay here for a little longer. "I'm sorry."

"You apologize too much," Miss Amanda said, waving her off the treadmill. "Looks like you're okay to head back up to your dorm. Just take it easy until you head home and come back down here immediately if there's anything that seems even a little strange. And back down here to check up tomorrow."

"Okay," Alice agreed. She got her things together and changed before heading up to her dorm room. Everyone was off at exams for the moment, which suited her fine because she had a completely different predicament to worry about at the moment.

She stumbled over one of the steps and pitched forward, catching herself on the rail. Footsteps from behind her came fast to help her up. "You okay?" he asked, Alice looking up to find Evan there.

"I'm fine," Alice said. "Just missed the step."

"Are you sure?"

"Yeah." Alice continued up the steps ahead of him to make the point, but she could feel the world starting to swim around her again. She made it all the way to her own room and let herself in, Evan following behind her and she left the door open if he wanted to come in for a visit. "I'm fine, you k now."

"I hear you aren't making it back next year," he said, sounding a little nervous.

"I know," she said. "I don't want to go."

Evan didn't say anything as Alice took a seat on her bed. She felt better now that she was sitting, but wasn't sure what to do with herself. The fact that she had to leave hadn't fully sunk in yet and she was still hopeful that something could happen to stop it. More than that, she hoped something would happen so she wouldn't have to try and convince her parents that she really remembered nothing.

"That's not really what I'm worried about," he finally said. "There was something the Bandersnatch said when you guys made that deal. He said when you *leave* middle school. You're leaving after all of this. And if you aren't coming back…"

Alice took a deep breath. "I know," she said. She realized that while she was stuck in that bed and found she wasn't nearly as scared about it as she should have been. "It might not be so bad, though. I mean, no one even remembered you when you were gone. No one's going to be sad I'm missing. I'll just be gone and then I won't have to worry about any of this other stuff anymore. No worrying about the Bandersnatch because he won. No more Cat. No more trying to save people in Wonderland. I won't be able to get Mark and Matt back, though. I'm sorry I didn't get them out first."

Evan fell quiet. That was probably all he wanted to talk

about. She reached between her mattresses and pulled out the brown book. At some point, she had the sense to put it back in its hiding spot before anyone tried to get their hands on it. The crumpled pages she'd caused during her captivity were flat now, like nothing had ever happened.

"This book has a whole bunch of stuff in it," she said, handing it to Evan. "None of it is going to work against the Bandersnatch anyway. But it's powerful and very dangerous. When I disappear, no one's going to be around to make sure it doesn't fall into the wrong hands. I don't want to make Adrianna do it, since she's not going to remember, but you might. Can you?"

Evan was quiet as he took it, flinching as he touched the cover. He sat down on Adrianna's bed and started to put it down on his lap before he thought better of it. He let it rest beside him instead. "Is that the book the Bandersnatch came out of?" he asked.

Alice nodded sadly and her eyes drifted to the cover. She should have never read that poem, no matter how much Cat had threatened her. She should have done something to stop all this. She could only hope the Jubjub birds would keep anyone else from going in there and sacrificing their friends for his promises. She couldn't handle more people getting forgotten because she was too stupid not to get caught in Wonderland for a month.

"Can you trade it?" Evan asked, looking back up at her. "You told him that it was the only thing you had, really, to get rid of him. Maybe you could trade him the book for undoing the last month. It'll be like when he put me back in everyone's memory. No one will even remember that you were gone."

Alice's heart jumped at the chance. There was only one problem. "I can't give up the book," Alice said. "There's all sorts of stuff in here that he could use. It could be danger-ous. And there's stuff I can use too that could come in really handy." It was also her only way to win the bet.

Evan took out his phone and put it down on Alice's desk. "Make a copy of it, then," he said. "Take a photo of all the pages and then give him the book. You can get it back from him when you manage to get rid of him for good."

Alice looked at the phone, then back to Evan. He was a genius. A kind and gentle genius. She was at a loss for words so she got up to hug him instead, tears starting to appear in her eyes. She kept them back as best she could, but she was certain Evan saw them anyway. After a moment, he patted her on the back and pulled away, meeting her eyes.

"You're going to be okay," he said. "You get it back to me somehow and I'll get the images of the pages to you. I'll email them over. And then you go and try to get that month of your life back."

He left her to start, Alice going through page by page and

taking photos as quickly and with as much detail as she could muster. She remembered the pages, but she was still anxious about handing the book over. There were more than just the three creatures contained in the pages and she was now essentially handing them over to the Bandersnatch. And all of her tricks. She was going to have to be very careful.

She finished and put the phone in her desk drawer with plenty of time to spare. She went to lay down on her bed, her mind going through the possibilities. If Evan was right, she would be fine. She could continue to go to school and keep trying to save Adrianna's brothers before the Bandersnatch's deadline. And she wouldn't really lose the book.

If this worked. She hoped this worked.

There was something outside her door and Alice sat up slowly at the sound. There were people out there, which was strange given where in the hall the room was. She waited, watching the door as Adrianna let herself in, hesitantly at first before her face broke into a huge smile.

"Alice!" she said, letting the door close behind her. She flung herself on Alice, wrapping her arms around her shoulders in a hug. "You weren't in the hospital wing anymore. Robert was worried your parents came and took you home before we got a chance to say goodbye."

"I'm still here," Alice said. She almost told Adrianna that she had a way to stay, but kept it to herself. She didn't want to get her hopes up. If it did work, Adrianna wouldn't even remember Alice had been gone at all. "I'm not going anywhere yet," she said instead. "How were exams?"

"Awful," Adrianna said, taking a seat next to her on her bed. "How do you feel? Are you okay? You want to get dinner?"

Alice shrugged. "A little dizzy still, but I'm okay. I don't think I can walk all the way to the cafeteria, though."

There was a knock at the door. Adrianna glanced at it and then back to Alice. "You think it's okay if everyone comes here?"

Alice smiled. "Did you get me dinner?"

Adrianna smiled broadly and opened the door. Heather came in first, holding up the spoils from the cafeteria, followed by Robert and Kevin. Heather dropped the bags on Adrianna's bed before she went over to scoop Alice up in a hug. She set Alice down and Alice stumbled on her feet.

"Sorry," Heather said, her hands out and ready to catch Alice if she fell.

Alice grabbed her shoulder to steady herself and let out a laugh. "It's okay," she said. "It's good to see you too. Sorry I made you guys so worried."

"God, stop apologizing!" Robert said. "After everything you've been through, you don't have anything to apologize for. You're just not allowed to do that anymore, okay?"

"Sorry," Alice said.

Robert let out a frustrated hum, but kept quiet. Kevin sat him down on the ground and they quickly fell into casual conversation as they set out the food between them on paper plates. Alice let them talk and was very glad when their only questions for her were about how she was feeling. They didn't ask what happened, though they were curious, and didn't even tell her what the rumours around her disappearance were. Instead, Heather kept them on track, focusing on what she missed in her time away.

"Robert desperately needs you to explain things," Heather said, looking like she was at her wits end. "He is seriously completely hopeless when it comes to all of this stuff."

"I am not!" he said. "Alice just tells it like it's a story instead of like it's just a bunch of names and treaties and battles and dates. You're just making history *more* boring when you try to explain it."

"That's because that's what we're getting *tested* on. The names and dates. That's what you have to know."

Alice smiled, glad she was missed but hoping that they wouldn't be there too long. "How's the play going?" she asked Heather and Kevin.

"He is killing it," Heather said before Kevin could try to be modest about anything. "He's picking up everything really fast and I think he's got half the damn thing memorized already. He's almost off book and everyone else is still just trying to keep up. I have no idea how he's doing it."

"I was in the play at my old school, that's all," he said. "I got some really good tips on picking stuff up quickly and how to flub things so it looks like you did it intentionally. It's no big deal."

"Don't let him tell you otherwise, he's doing amazing."

"You know, you'd probably be off book and everything too if you weren't in a billion different clubs, Heather," Robert said. "I'm surprised you weren't down there with Alice near the end."

Alice smiled as Heather gave Robert a light swat. It was good to know life went on fine without her. And hopefully, everything would be perfectly normal sooner if all went well tonight.

CHAPTER 17

The Bandersnatch's Bargain

SHE WAITED UNTIL Adrianna was asleep before she got out of bed and changed to leave again. She was tired now, not used to the late nights anymore, but it would be fine. This was the last one for a good while, since she had absolutely no intention of actually going into Wonderland for a long time. At least, not until she figured out a way to avoid Tiger Lily.

In a few steps she was across campus, in the woods and then in the depths of the fog. The effort tired her and Alice needed to stop in the midst of not being able to see anything to catch her breath and wait for everything to stop spinning. After a moment, she continued to walk into the Bandersnatch's lair.

The Bandersnatch decorated his lair in more of everything she didn't like. It was more silver and metal now, shiny and elegant. The ground was covered in a thick layer of frosted ice.

She clutched the book in hand and the Bandersnatch appeared before her.

"Hello, Alice," he said, smiling widely. His form was tall, but it shrunk down into a creature only a little larger than her, the darkness in the area spreading so that it was darker than usual. "What a lovely surprise. You were only just released from the hospital today. I am quite surprised you wanted to see me already. Although, I think I know why you might be here. Come to try and banish me before you leave the school?"

"No," Alice told him.

He grinned. "No?" he asked. "Well isn't this interesting. Here to accept your defeat, then?" He sauntered up closer to her, staring at her with those four white eyes.

"I want to make a deal," she said. "I want everyone to forget about the last month while I was gone. I want people to think I was here and everything was normal."

"Hm," the Bandersnatch said, wrapping her in darkness and coming out taller beside her. "I see that you haven't brought anyone to bargain with. So tell me, Alice dear, what do you propose you trade to complete this proposition?"

"The book," she said. "I'll give you the book."

The Bandersnatch pulled back and took a long, appraising look at her. "You would be willing to sacrifice your only hope at winning our little bet for a little more time with your friends and your life?" He was amused at the prospect and he seemed to be considering it.

"I can think of another way," Alice said, though she was not confident. "I'll think of something. I just need a little more time. Please."

The Bandersnatch hovered over her for a moment, then it all went dark. When the light came back again, he was sitting on his throne with the book and Alice sat on the chair in front of him. "You have a deal. Trading my prison and your only hope to win our little bet is a risky move, child. You know you have no hope left of our other deal now."

"I'll think of something," Alice said. She was getting very tired, but refrained from yawning as best she could.

"I'm counting on that," the Bandersnatch said. "It would be terribly dull if you failed before you even tried anything. But with this book in my hands, it is not quite enough. I think limiting your hero status once more is in order until you leave the grounds next."

"But—" Alice started, but she didn't want to make him angry after they had just made the deal and he thought they were still negotiating. "I mean, the last time, Wonderland slipped back through. Cat made it through and—"

"Ah yes, that," he said, the white in his eyes narrowing as if he were smiling. "That is the risk you will have to take.

Now, return to your bed. And be sure to make this game interesting for me from now on."

WHEN ALICE WOKE up in the morning, she was feeling significantly better. She had dreamed a very different last month than she had actually had, one where she had actually been in school instead of stuck in that tent. She wasn't being kept from coming back next year at all and she'd actually taken her finals with everyone else. It was a lovely dream.

Adrianna was already up and looking confused as she got ready. She didn't say anything to Alice as she got up, but Adrianna looked like she knew that something very strange had happened. After a while of quiet between the pair of them, she turned to Alice.

"Can I ask you something really weird?" she asked "Like, really weird?"

"Sure," Alice said, though she was actually shrinking inside at the question. "What is it?"

"Last month is all kind of weird," she said. "I remember it where you were here all month and I remember it where you were gone. It's getting harder to remember it when you were gone now, though. And usually I'd just think I dreamed you being gone for a month and it's hard to remember like it was a dream, but it really happened, didn't it? You were gone?"

Alice couldn't stop herself from smiling. "It worked?" she asked.

"What worked?"

"I..." Alice had to stop herself, trying to come up with the words and put them all together before she actually spoke. "I was gone," she said at last. "I was gone for a whole month. And then, when I got back, I found out my parents weren't going to let me come back and people kept asking questions and I was going to leave. So I made a deal with the Bandersnatch."

"Alice!" Adrianna said, horrified. "You gave someone to the Bandersnatch?"

"No!" Alice said. "No, I wouldn't do that. I just gave him the book."

"I guess that's better," Adrianna said, though she was still apprehensive. "But don't you need that? I mean, the Jabberwocky is still in Wonderland and doing stuff there, right? And that was how you were going to get the Bandersnatch to leave. How are you going to do all that if the Bandersnatch has the book? There's no way to get rid of him without it."

"There's no way to get rid of him with it," Alice told her grimly. "And it's okay. I used Evan's phone to make a copy of all the pages. I just need to hope he doesn't delete them all and sends them back to me. Oh, that reminds me," she said, going to her desk drawer. The phone was still there, as was an archive of photos that looked very much like the brown book. She passed it back to Adrianna. "Can you give this back to him?"

"Yeah," Adrianna said, smiling. "You could probably give it to him yourself, though."

"What do you mean?"

"I got word from my dad yesterday. Your dad said it was okay if you came to spend Christmas with us this year!"

"Really?" Alice was in shock. Not only did she get her month back, but she was also getting to go home with Adrianna for Christmas? For a moment she hoped that she wasn't going to miss Lori if she went home for the holidays, but her parents wouldn't let her go if Lori was coming back. She knew they wouldn't.

Adrianna smiled. "Really! It's going to be so much fun."

Alice was happy about all of this and she did nothing to hide her excitement from Adrianna. They still, however, had things to do. They weren't quite done with school yet, with the dance still happening tonight, and Adrianna had one last choir practice to make before the end of the year.

When she was alone, Alice looked in the mirror, trying to make it turn into a way to Wonderland. Nothing. The Bandersnatch said he would take something away from her until she visited again, and this was probably it. That was fine by her. She would go back eventually, but for now she needed a break from the place.

She was about to turn away and go back to her day when a pair of purple eyes stared back at her. Wonderland appeared behind him and Alice leaned forward, her fingers brushing the cool glass of the mirror and not going through. On the other side, the Cheshire Cat appeared in the scene, standing on the ground and grinning at her.

"You look well," he said, twitching. It seemed the effects of the tent were still getting to him.

"As do you," Alice said tightly. "Hello Cat. Will you be coming back to send more of my friends through with you?"

"My way out seems to have escaped itself," he said. "Don't think I won't find another way."

"I'll be waiting," Alice said. Cat vanished, leaving the image of Wonderland fading away into a reflection again, but in the distance she saw something very strange. She squinted at the trees in the distance. There was a boy who looked very much like Mike holding a book and floating down from the sky and into the treetops.

She tried to go through, but her hand hit the mirror. Finally, a sign of one of them. At least now she had a place to start looking.

About the Author

TANYA LISLE IS a novelist from the Metro Vancouver, British Columbia, who has series littered across genres from supernatural horror to young adult fantasy. She began writing in elementary school, when she started turning homework assignments into short stories and continued this trend well into university. While attending Simon Fraser University, she developed an appreciation for public domain crossovers and cross-platform narratives. She has a shelf full of notebooks with more story ideas than pens lost to the depths of her bag. Now she writes incessantly in hopes of finishing all of them.

Thankfully, her cat, Remy, has figured out how to shut off Tanya's computer when she needs to take a break.